FORGING THE SWORD

THE FOOTNAIL SERIES – BOOK 2

A.K. HOWARD

Forging the Sword

ISBN (Paperback): 978-1-990678-11-0
ISBN (eBook): 978-1-990678-10-3

PROLOGUE

CONSTANTINOPLE, 327 A.D.

The darkness was closing in, trying to hedge Queen Helena on every side.

She tried to hide the weariness on her face as she descended a narrow staircase holding a torch in her hand. Her Praetorian guards—four of the best she had—surrounded her.

Four of the best she had.

Their leader walked a few feet ahead. He moved briskly; an air of confidence surrounding him as his eyes roamed every dark corner before Helena reached them.

She didn't cherish what she had to do, but it was inevitable. She returned from her pilgrimage to Jerusalem to find the capital in unrest, and she had spent the past three weeks trying to stop one faction or the other from creating chaos.

Her journey hadn't been easy. The accursed tried to kill her; their very name was like a bitter pill she had to swallow. They were powerful, and they were after her, or rather, after the holy artifact she possessed.

Her last pilgrimage to the holy land had unearthed something; something miraculous.

The tree nails used in the crucifixion of Jesus Christ of Nazareth.

She hadn't known that four immortals, cursed to wander the earth for eternity, were also after the nails, and the discovery started a deadly cat and mouse game. The accursed desired the nails to set themselves free from the curse, but Queen Helena needed them to keep safe her last remaining precious possession—her son.

She would turn the world upside down if it meant her son would continue to rule as emperor.

Much rested on him, and he could only play his part if he was safe and in power. Forces rose to topple his rule, and she would do everything in her power to stop them.

Helena reached the bottom of the stairs.

The smell of wet moss and mold filled the air. This section of the palace was rarely visited. She didn't know about it until a night ago, when Calisto, the head of her guards, informed her of an assassin trying to infiltrate the sacred palace.

Down here was a cell with a door made from thick wood.

"This bloody bolt must be rusty," one of the guards grunted as he pulled its bolt back.

Calisto stayed by Helena's side while the other three guards entered the cell.

Helena took a moment to appraise her bodyguard. He stood alert in his leather tunic, a white-knuckled hand clutching the pommel of his sword. Calisto was bred for battle, and he exuded a keen sense of danger wherever he went. He caught Helena's stone-cold brown eyes looking at him and grinned. She would have found it alluring if she was thirty years younger. Now she found his smirk irritating.

Helena walked in, and Calisto followed closely behind.

It was the size of a monk's cell; she could stretch out her arms and touch both walls. The damp crawled up her spine like an army of ants and mixed with it was the overpowering metallic smell of age-old blood.

This was a torture chamber.

Helena's torch cast a hard shadow across the tiny cell, providing just enough light to reveal the slumped outline of a prisoner.

Helena examined him closer and was relieved to see that he looked mostly intact, given the circumstances. Chains that sunk into the ground at each corner of the cell secured his hands and feet. He had a scruffy beard that partially covered a deep cut across his cheek, and he emitted an acrid mix of sweat and body odor. Clearly, he had been roughed up a bit, but Helena knew it could have been worse.

"Ah, finally," he whispered weakly, "she blesses us with her glorious presence."

He opened his eyes, which swirled with a darkness only Queen Helena could see, and she stumbled back.

She had seen that same darkness when Marius, one of the accursed after her and the nails, tried to kill her on the road to Constantinople. He had possessed her guards, and the only outward sign they were no longer in control of their own minds were their vacant, black eyes.

"He is possessed," she said, trying to still her rapidly beating heart. The air sizzled with tension as her guards clenched their swords in anticipation.

All they needed was one command, and blood would flow.

Amid the prone guards, Calisto looked calmly. "It seems Marius is becoming a pain in the backside," he said.

Helena grunted in agreement. Marius' ability to influence people's minds and take over their bodies had ended with Calisto. He had tried, and succeeded for a time, but Calisto had somehow broken the spell and became immune.

Others weren't so successful; they became puppets in the hands of a puppet master.

"I bring a message for your ears, oh Queen."

Helena knew the sound of that voice, and it didn't belong to the prisoner chained to the ground. The voice belonged to a slim, athletic man who imagined himself a gentleman but was nothing more than a scoundrel and a coward.

Well, a coward with the ability to manipulate people according to his wishes.

"Speak," Helena said.

"Give me what is mine, and I will let you live. Withhold, and your people will suffer. I will find those you hold dear and cause them to commit the most atrocious acts. You will watch as your dear Christians are killed. Be wise and do the right thing."

The prisoner slumped when he finished speaking, and for a moment, Helena thought he was dead, but he slowly raised his head and looked around.

"Where...what is... going on? Where am I?" Dribble trailed down the corner of the prisoner's mouth as he noticed the chains and jerked forward. He suddenly noticed Helena. "Mother Empress! Help me."

Helena stepped forward, but Calisto held her arm and stopped her.

"We can't be sure it's safe, my Queen."

"His eyes are clear, Calisto. He isn't possessed anymore."

"Aye, but what if that's his plan? We do not know enough about Marius, and the wizard isn't here with us. Caution is the only acceptable choice."

Helena looked at the prisoner with anguish in her heart. Calisto was right. They didn't know the extent of Marius's powers, and Merlin wasn't there to counter any spell or magic.

"What is the last thing you remember, Legionary?" Calisto asked.

"I was on patrol with my unit when a man approached us. We ordered him to identify himself, but he only laughed. All of a sudden, I heard a voice commanding me to stand still, and I found myself obeying. I watched as the others in my unit killed themselves. The man walked up to me and told me to deliver a message. After that…I don't seem to remember anything else."

"It's him," Helena voiced confidently.

Calisto nodded. "We will keep him here for a couple of days to be sure."

Calisto saw the look on Queen Helena's face and quickly added, "He will be comfortable, and he won't be hurt. It's only a precautionary measure, but a necessary one."

Helena reluctantly agreed.

She nodded reluctantly and walked to the cell door, glancing over her shoulder to take a last look at the prisoner, who still had a bewildered look on his face.

The attack on his unit was the most recent by the accursed. The one before had been an attempt to burn a local gathering of Christians gathered at a believer's house. Somehow, Marius seemed unable to control Christians, but that didn't stop him from harming them through others.

She made her way back up the stairs with Calisto, arriving in a sparsely furnished room with a bed and chair.

Calisto ordered two guards to stay behind and escorted Queen Helena out of the house.

On the street, Calisto slowed his pace to match Queen Helena's, still glancing around for the tiniest sign of trouble. The night was quiet; a cool breeze caressed his cheeks as he they walked. Calisto needed a win. He was tired of reacting to the enemy's attacks; they wouldn't win that way. He itched to get his hands or, better still, his sword through one of those damned, cursed individuals.

Knowing the layout of the palace and surrounding neighborhood well, he walked instinctively. He had accompanied the queen on her visits to numerous houses here and was aware of where the beggars gathered and where the pickpockets made their gains.

On a typical day, he wouldn't have been concerned about bringing her here; the people loved and admired her. Most would protect her with their lives. But the wormwood had made that impossible. Now he couldn't trust anybody. Any man's friendly smile could conceal the fact that he carried a knife, and nearness could mean sudden death.

Helena knew the dangers and let him have free rein. For that, Calisto was grateful. It made protecting her easier.

They reached the palace without incident, and Calisto escorted the queen to her private chambers, nodding to the two guards posted outside. They stood alert with their hands gripping their spears by their sides.

"Report."

"Nothing unusual, Champion."

Calisto grunted. His brothers-in-arms were the only ones privileged to call him by that name. They had bled and died with him; served numerous campaigns, and he felt honored to be their leader.

As he swung open the door, Calisto heard the rhythmic sound of synchronized feet approaching from behind. He turned to see the emperor of Rome and the whole civilized world marching in their direction within a large group of men.

"Imperator Augustus!"

The guards slammed their fists to their chests in greeting as Emperor Constantine the Great approached Queen Helena. He was clean-shaven and wore a deep purple robe with a crimson hem.

"I hope I did not catch you at an inconvenient time, Mother," he smiled, hugging Helena.

"What brings you here at this time? I hope all is well?"

Calisto studied the group. Constantine's entourage consisted of politicians, members of the sacrum consistorium, and personal advisers. Among them was Thaddeus, the Master of Offices, and Cassius, the spymaster.

Calisto frowned. The emperor's presence wasn't mere cordiality. Queen Helena seemed to know this too, her posture tensed and she steepled her fingers as she listened to her son.

"Mother, I know you listen to Hyginos, and for that, I have stayed my hand, but he has begun to speak against me. He has to stop."

"I don't understand. Why would he do that? He supports you and has always done so."

"And that is why I'm here, Mother. He now speaks vehemently against the empire in his gatherings, inciting the people to violence against the throne."

It made no sense. Hyginos was a man of peace, a Christian who believed in the good her son was doing. He had greatly rejoiced when the *Nicene Creed* had been instituted. Why would he turn on the empire?

"I'll talk to him at first light."

Emperor Constantine nodded and strode away.

"Where is that blasted wizard when we need him?" Helena muttered to Calisto when they were out of earshot. "I perceive the hand of the accursed in trying to stir trouble."

"What do you want me to do?" Calisto asked, following Helena into her private room.

She brushed aside greetings from her maids and clapped her hands in irritation. "Leave us!"

The women hurried to obey, and within minutes they were alone, only the guards outside the door remaining nearby.

"Now, the threat from the prisoner makes sense," Helena stated.

Calisto nodded in agreement. He had figured that out the moment the emperor had expressed his displeasure. The question now was if he should kill him.

Helena noticed the determined look in his eyes and shook her head. "Violence won't work here,

Calisto. We have to be subtle. If it is one of the accursed, we need to understand what he wants."

"It's obvious, Empress," he said as he moved closer. "They want the nails. They will continue to apply pressure until you give in. We cannot afford that."

"No, we cannot. But we cannot allow them to tarnish the Christians and bring about the persecutions again."

Merlin watched the street from the doorway of a small, thatched house. Though it was late, people walked down the street in pairs and groups, and he avoided their notice by blending into the shadows in his simple, dark clothes.

Constantinople was safe, as safe as Emperor Constantine's city could be. Crime wasn't nonexistent; Merlin caught the occasional glint of firelight on reflective metal of patrolling guards' swords.

Merlin concentrated on four men making their way down the street. He had been trailing them for a while now, following them from inn to inn as they conversed with clients and other unsavory characters.

He knew the type, but something about these four seemed off. They never drank too much, and though they staggered down the street, Merlin wasn't fooled. He knew they were sober and vigilant.

And so, Merlin waited.

He needed to find the source of the disturbances in the city. Someone was fueling the citizens against the government and casting the blame on local Christians. While Merlin was sure the accursed were behind the dastardly attempt, his gut told him they had willing accomplices among the people of Constantinople. Hearts could be easily swayed—especially when there was the promise of fame and wealth.

The four men headed into a house at the end of the street, so Merlin waited a couple of seconds and then stepped out of the doorway.

At the door, he quickly muttered a spell and it swung open silently. Looking both ways to ensure no one was watching, he entered.

Inside, the four men were waiting for him. Up close, Merlin could see their weathered, sunburnt faces, and he assumed they were seafarers or sailors. One had a scar across the bridge of his nose, while another batted his palm with a cudgel. They had one thing in common—an arcane drawing carved into their foreheads.

"We smelled you miles away, wizard," the man with the cudgel spat.

"And we'll rough you up," the scar-faced thug added.

Merlin shook his head. They were all muscles, no brains. If they had any intelligence, they would have been wary of someone they claimed was a wizard.

"Who do you work for?" Merlin asked. Maybe they would be dumb enough to tell him.

"What do you take us for?" Scar Face asked.

"Simpletons?" Cudgel Wielder finished.

Merlin glanced at the other two, who had been silent, and felt his skin tingle as he locked eyes with one of them. The man was rail-thin, with a skull-like face and bloodshot eyes. The mark on his forehead glowed red for a moment, and he stretched out his hands toward Merlin and screamed, "Pyrkagia!"

Fire blossomed from the man's hand and rushed toward Merlin, who spun and reached out, grabbing the flames. Squeezing his hand into a fist, he snuffed them out.

"Let us try that again; who do you work for?"

The four men stared with their mouths agape. Cudgel Wielder glanced from Merlin to the door and back to Merlin. Scar Face was the first to shrug off his fear and pull out a long, sharp knife. He screamed defiantly and rushed, causing the other three to find their courage and attack with him, hoping superiority in numbers would give them an advantage.

They didn't know who stood before them.

A blast of wind threw them back, and they slammed against the wall. The raging wind swirling in the small room Kept them pinned back, and they wailed in fear.

Merlin felt the lethal urge snapping at his heels, but he forced down the desire and cut off the wind in an instant.

Air was easy to manipulate. He had sworn never to use the other elements, as they were wilder and required better control. Not that he *couldn't* control them; he had used fire and earth for eons, and they responded to his call faster, but they also pushed him to the brink of reasoning.

The four scrambled to the edge of the room in an attempt to get as far away as possible.

"What cult do you follow, and what are your plans?" Merlin demanded.

"We are ready to die. We will never tell," Skull Face sneered, but fear was eroding their attempt at bravado. Merlin pointed at the men.

"We don't know anything about any cult. We were paid," Cudgel Wielder blurted.

"Silence, fool," Skull Face demanded.

Merlin flicked his finger, and the air surrounding Skull Face was sucked away. He grabbed at his throat, his face grew pale, and he passed out a moment later.

Merlin turned his attention on the remaining three men, who flinched backward. He released his hold on the air around Skull Face, and he saw that the man was breathing, but his fellow thugs weren't aware of that.

"We don't know his name," Scar Face shouted as Cudgel Wielder, and the remaining member of the group nodded in agreement.

"He paid us to go around defaming the emperor. That's all we know. He told us to obey Aetius over there," Scar Face nodded toward Skull Face on the ground.

"How do you meet this man?"

"We don't. A messenger drops an address for the next meeting point. The messenger is never the same person."

"What does the man who paid you look like?"

"We don't know. We've never seen his face. He wears a hood all the time or remains in the dark. I'm telling the truth; please don't kill us."

Merlin was already heading to the door. "Make sure you are out of this city by first light, or your lives are forfeited," he called over his shoulder, and strode out of the house.

Could it be the accursed stirring trouble for the emperor? Or did they have another contender in this deadly game?

1

"**C**an you follow my finger, please?"

Gen nodded. The doctor's hand moved to her left and right, just inches from her face.

She couldn't see the finger, and yet at the same time, she could.

Ever since the incident at the hospital, her world had turned to one of white, black, and grey tones. Colours didn't precisely define what she saw; everything was shades.

She saw the doctor as an image on an old black and white television, without fine details like the buttons on his white coat.

Though she knew she was in a doctor's office, she couldn't make out any specifics. There was a desk, and he sat on the edge of it while examining her. His large outline revealed that he had a head, body, hands, and feet, but she couldn't tell if he was white or black or any race, for that matter. She didn't know if he had small eyes and a huge nose.

"Mmmm. I must confess, this is extremely baffling," he said. The timbre of his voice made him sound young. "The tests all came back negative."

Gen couldn't blame him for his hesitation and slightly skeptical tone.

Two weeks ago, she could see perfectly. Then, right in this very hospital, she had called on a power deep within herself, and the result was this freakish new sight.

"But?" Gen prompted.

"Eh, you don't have pupils or irises. You should be blind. Scientifically, you shouldn't be able to see anything."

The doctor coughed to hide his discomfort. Gen refrained from telling him that she could see something even deeper than normal vision.

The essence, or the soul, of everything around her was now visible. Every object in the office emitted a type of shimmering light that only she could see. To her eyes, there was a radius of white energy at the centre of every living thing. Some shone brighter than others, their whites so bright that it hurt the eyes to look directly at them. Some had specks of darkness, and a few, a tiny few, emitted darkness so black that it sucked at the light around them.

Gen had met a couple of people in the last category, and one had tried to kill her. That was the incident at the hospital a couple of weeks ago.

"So, what next?"

"We...eh, book another appointment. Come back in two weeks, and we'll do another checkup."

Gen nodded but sighed inwardly. She knew there was nothing the doctor could do, but her parents had pressured her into coming. They were worried that something could be wrong with her, and she had been unwilling to tell them otherwise.

She saw the doctor stretch out his hand and, though she saw only the outline, she tried not to smile as she grasped it with a firm handshake. She didn't need to see his expression; she heard the sound of surprise from his mouth.

Outside his office, she brought out a pair of sunglasses and ignored the stares she was sure she was getting. Her parents were in the waiting room. Her mum sat with her hands resting gently on her knees—the figure of elegance. She was in her forties and had greying hair but looked ten years younger. Gen's father beside her was a complete contrast. His hair looked ruffled, but her mum didn't have a strand out of place. He sat casually with a hand draped over his wife's shoulders.

Standing beside them, leaning casually on the wall with a nonchalant look, was her protector, Mark Reynolds. Mark's indifferent stance didn't fool Gen. She felt a throbbing power emanating from him. He looked ready to attack anything and anyone that threatened her.

Gen didn't need her sight to remember what Mark looked like; his features were engraved in her heart and soul. She knew him, and now her inner sight revealed him even better.

The last figure—a tall, slim man in his late fifties—paced the narrow corridor, his usually smiling face twisted into a worried frown. Her grandfather and mentor. Even though he wasn't related to her by blood, he had been instrumental in bringing her up and would always be her grandfather.

This was her family.

They had shed blood together, and one had literally given his life for her—twice.

They all shone with a light that was bright and filled with love and affection toward her.

She could sense their worry as she approached. Well, Mark didn't seem fazed by her new appearance, which he chalked up to his new ability to sense magic.

Gen's parents sprang to their feet and rushed to her side.

"What did the doctor say, honey?" her mum asked.

Gen smelt her mum's familiar vanilla-scented perfume as her mum stood by her side.

"That there's nothing wrong with me."

"Did he run any tests? Sometimes they forget to run tests."

"He ran tests, Mum. I think he knows how to do his job."

"He looked too young to be a doctor. Maybe we should get a second opinion?"

"Let her be, dear." Gen's father patted his wife's arm.

"I think this is a discussion for the ranch," her grandfather suggested.

Her mum opened her mouth to say something but thought better of it and kept quiet. Gen smiled and turned to Mark.

"What's your take, Mark?"

Mark pushed himself off the wall and shrugged. "Love the glasses."

Gen laughed and hooked her arm through her mother's. She didn't understand why Mark's opinion mattered to her, but it did. They had been through so much together in such a short time, and she had come to care for him a great deal.

They drove back to the Triple 7 ranch in comfortable silence. Gen was wedged between Mark and her grandfather in the back of the van, feeling safe and secure, while her parents took the front seats.

Mark was ex-special forces and ran a security outfit. Not only that, but he now had the memories of his ancestor, who had also been a protector and knew more about combat than most men alive.

And then, there was her grandfather. He was an immortal and an extremely powerful magician who had been known by many names over the millennia, the most famous of which was Merlin. Gen had known him as Melvin Gourdeau, and his real name was Myrddin Emrys Wylit.

Sometimes she still found it hard to accept that the kind and simple-looking man beside her was the great Merlin, practically a legend, an elder in the world of magicians.

Between the two of them, Gen was confident they could handle anything.

Suddenly, the world around her disappeared, and she saw herself elsewhere. She was used to her visions by now, so she wasn't surprised. What did startle her was that it was occurring without her touching the nail. The foot nail that was used to crucify Jesus Christ had come into her possession and brought vivid visions of the life of Christ with it. ·

Gen tried to get her bearings. She was in some sort of building, maybe a temple. There was a large crowd gathered in the courtyard just ahead of her, and they seemed to be arguing. She walked toward them and let their words wash over her. They were meaningless to her, but she knew from past experience that the language would soon become understandable.

"...we are Abraham's seed and are not slaves to any man. What do you mean by saying, 'if we know the truth, the truth shall set us free'?"

Gen stopped at the fringe of the crowd, where there were mutterings of agreement.

"Truly, I tell you that anyone that commits sin is a servant to sin. The servant doesn't reside in the house forever, but the son does. If the son makes you free...you are truly free."

Gen knew enough to understand that those words were the purpose of her vision. Jesus wanted her to remember them.

Was she truly free? What did it even mean to be free?

She pondered the concept as the world flashed white.

Gen returned to see that time hadn't passed in the world. She still sat between Mark and her grandfather.

Mark turned to her and smiled. "Penny for your thoughts?"

"I could ask the same of you. You seem to be handling this "girl suddenly loses sight" thing pretty calmly," she teased.

"Did a tour in Iraq," Mark said. "Had a corporal who believed his girlfriend's picture was his lucky charm. Went with it everywhere, and I mean everywhere."

"What happened?" Gen prompted when he remained silent for a while.

"Oh, he survived and was discharged a couple of years later."

"So, it worked?"

"Don't know if it worked or not, but people believe in all sorts of things to get by. You brought me back from the dead, Gen. Don't care if you've got white eyes or purple eyes. I'm with you to the end."

Gen stared at Mark in amazement. That was the longest speech he'd ever made, and she had felt every word.

"I just had a vision."

Myrddin turned and looked at her.

"Without the nail?"

She nodded.

"And you're sure it's…you know, the same?" Mark asked.

Gen raised an eyebrow. "I think by now I should be an expert on these visions. It's the same. Jesus was in a temple; there was an argument. I couldn't get through the crowd, but I heard Him say something about setting people free."

"Do you remember the exact words?" Myrddin asked.

"Might not be able to say it word for word, but He said something like, 'If the son makes you free, you are truly free.'"

"Who was He talking about?" Mark knew the visions were real, he had seen Gen experience one, but he still couldn't quite get around the fact that Gen was seeing Jesus Christ.

"He's talking about Himself, Mark." Gen looked at Mark oddly. "That statement means if Jesus Christ sets you free, you are free indeed. Didn't you go to Sunday school?"

"No. My father never had an interest in his kids' spirituality."

"He was talking about spiritual freedom from the way the religious body of that time thought and operated," Myrddin explained.

"That's the Pharisees, right?" Gen asked.

"Among others."

"But what type of freedom are we talking about?" Mark wondered.

"I think the real question we should be asking is why this particular vision. The visions have always had a purpose, so what's the purpose of this one?" Myrddin thought aloud.

"And why can she have the visions without touching the nail?" Mark added.

Gen watched as they both turned to look at her, and she shrugged.

How was she supposed to know the answer?

They arrived at the ranch some minutes later, and Gen took a second to look at her home. It had seen better days, but that wasn't what made it special.

She had grown up in Dundurn, a tiny town with a population in the hundreds. Everybody knew everybody; there was a sense of real community. She was brought up mostly by her grandfather, and though she now knew the reason why, she was still grateful for the love he had shown her.

The Triple 7 ranch had once bred horses and still had a barn at the corner of the land. The main house loomed into view as Gen's father parked the van, and everyone climbed out.

Everything looked peaceful, a sharp contrast to two weeks ago when they were all fighting for their lives against the accursed, a group of immortals bent on killing Gen and taking the nail for themselves. The only testament to the destruction wrought was the front door.

It was new, and its fresh and shiny, red-painted wood stood in sharp contrast to the house's texture. The last door had been blown to smithereens by Atticus, one of the accursed.

Myrddin assured them that the new door was impregnable and fortified with one of his spells.

Gen smiled as Mark walked to her side. She reached out and took his hand, interlocking her fingers with his. For some days now, her spirit had been uneasy, and she sensed something was coming. She wasn't sure what it was, but she knew that with Mark and her family by her side, she could take on the world.

Isabella turned off the ignition and picked up her handbag from the passenger seat. She rummaged through it until she found her tape recorder, notebook, and pen—essential tools for a girl in the field.

A couple rushed by as she stepped out of the car, and she quickly stepped out of their way before walking to the hospital's entrance.

At the front desk, a young woman looked up from the computer and smiled at her.

"Hello, I'm Isabella from the *Daily Sun* and—"

"Gina! Got another one," the young receptionist called out to a tall, black woman by the printer. She stepped to the desk, where the first woman pushed a file toward her. Gina scanned its contents before peering at Isabella.

"What's the problem?" Gina asked.

"As I was telling your...second over there, I'm from the *Daily Sun,* and I'd like to ask some questions..."

"Regarding the miracles that occurred here? Ain't you a little late?" Gina chuckled.

"Miracles? Is that what you're calling them?"

"What else do you call an extremely sick person getting up from their hospital bed and going home cured?"

"Coincidence?"

"And when it happens to every sick person?" Isabella opened her mouth to answer, but Gina continued. "... at the same time?"

Isabella shut her mouth.

She had followed the news on television, but the theory of something spectacular happening had been debunked by reputable doctors. The whole thing was an exaggeration, they said.

"That's not what was reported," Isabella said.

"But that's what happened. I was right here that night. The whole corridor lit up, and moments later, people were getting healed left, right, and centre."

"And did any agree to be interviewed?"

"They did, but you reporters say and write what you want. Never seen people so dumb."

Isabella took the insult in her stride. She had heard worse. "Is there anyone here who can corroborate your story?"

"Not anymore. Haven't you been listening?" Gina rolled her eyes and gave a look that reminded Isabella of her grandmother when she thought she was asking stupid questions. "They all got healed and left. Went home to their respective lives."

"Okay, so, what was the most…eh, what case stood out to you?"

"Oh, that's easy. Josephine Baddock. Was dying of terminal cancer. Got healed just like that." Gina snapped her fingers so suddenly that Isabella almost jumped back.

"She had cancer?"

"Are you dumb or something? I just said that, didn't I?"

"Just making sure I heard you right."

Isabella stepped aside for a nurse wheeling past with a gurney carrying a groaning patient.

"You heard me right. She was bedridden and didn't have long to live. Can tell you, it was an eyeopener seeing her walk out of the hospital on her two feet."

Isabella tried not to stomp her own feet in excitement. If somehow, someone had a riveting story to tell, that could get her through certain doors. She looked around and saw a woman in dark sunglasses walk up to a group, presumably her family. She watched them for a minute before turning back to Gina, who was flipping through a file on the counter.

"So, can I have Josephine's number?"

Gina burst into laughter and shook her head. "Can't do that."

"If this woman has something to say—"

"Not gonna happen."

Gina turned back to the printer, making clear their conversation was over. Isabella wasn't discouraged; she had something any good reporter could build on: she had a name.

2

en walked into the kitchen, where Mark sat by the table with a cup of coffee in his hand. He smiled at her. "How was your night?"

She grimaced as she trudged to the coffee maker. Her night had been restless. She poured herself a coffee and turned to see Mark looking at her over the rim of his steaming cup.

"Couldn't sleep." She walked to the table and sat beside him. "Remember that vision about the wheat field and the seven of us? The one I had about two weeks ago?"

"Yes."

"Well, I had the same vision last night."

"The exact same one?"

"Well, maybe not image for image, but basically the same thing. Been trying to figure out what that could mean."

"Well, whatever it means, we have to take it seriously. For you to have the same vision twice is unnerving."

Gen nodded.

She had the vision when she saved Mark's life, or rather, brought him back from the dead. It was about her protecting a wheat field from a great darkness.

Between the two of them and Myrddin, they agreed that the wheat field represented humanity, and that she was meant to save it from a great evil. There were two members of the accursed left out there somewhere, and wherever they went, death and destruction followed. Gen didn't think there was any other evil greater than them.

"What if we're going about it the wrong way?" Mark wondered aloud.

"What do you mean?" Gen said, taking a sip of her coffee.

"We've always assumed that the vision was a metaphor, you know, the 'you saving the whole world' thing."

Gen shifted uncomfortably. The whole "saviour of humanity" thing made her wary.

"What if we're meant to take the vision literally?" he continued. "Hold on, hear me out," he added hastily when he saw the look on Gen's face.

"We know that the wheat field means the world or the people. I remember Myrddin's lecture on the parable of the sower, and from a logical point of view, it makes sense. But what if the people you saw were real? That's the part that's been nagging at the back of my brain ever since you mentioned the vision. Hearing it again just clicked for me. What if the seven people are symbolic or real or whatever?"

That's right, Gen thought in excitement.

That's what made the vision important. She needed help from others.

"How did you come up with this?" she grinned.

"I have my moments."

Gen felt her heart lurch.

Why did she have to react to him this way? She knew she had feelings for him, and sometimes, she felt the intensity of his gaze wash over her and make her feel warm all over.

Her new sight didn't help matters; he stood like a sun in her eyes. He radiated honour and loyalty, which she assumed were from his role as her protector, but sometimes she even detected love directed at her when she wasn't looking.

"So, how do we find these people?" Gen defused the moment before it sucked her in completely. She felt Mark switch gears mentally, becoming the professional security expert, and she felt a little sad.

"Can you remember their faces?"

"I think so. One or two are more vivid in my mind than others."

"Then we need to do something quickly before you forget. We need a sketch artist."

Gen sighed. She knew who could help out in that regard.

"We need to go into town."

Theo Cuttaham glanced at the empty seat across from his desk. The sheriff's office looked too large without Dundurn's chief sat there. His presence had somehow been the epicentre of their little space. Theo swung his feet up on his desk and tried to relax. He was in charge now. Maybe it would help to rearrange the two desks that comprised more than half of the furniture in the office?

He heard a vehicle cruise to a stop outside, and his heart felt as though someone was squeezing it with a fist.

Nothing to be afraid of, Theo pacified his agitated state.

He remembered the man who walked into this office a couple of weeks ago, and the world of pain and anguish he brought with him. An image of his father slumped and broken on the ground at the Triple 7 ranch flashed through his mind, and his hand instinctively moved to his revolver.

He watched the door open slowly, then breathed a sigh of relief when he saw Genesis Isherwood walk in. Behind her was Mark Reynolds, a sentient shadow that always seemed to be by her side nowadays.

Gen's smile wavered when she saw the flushed and scared look on Theo's face. She had her sunglasses on, so she knew she couldn't be the source of terror that she had seen on his face.

"Theo?"

"Gen. What brings you here?"

She studied Theo's face. Though she could only see in shades of white and grey, Theo was a childhood friend. He always had a boyish grin and looks that belied his age; she remembered teasing him for it countless times when they were growing up.

Mark had taken a casual stride to the left of the room. Gen knew him well enough now to understand his thinking: he was standing in a way that meant he could intercept Theo should he prove to be a threat while at the same time observing the door. She also knew he carried a gun behind his back, holstered in a belt and underneath his checkered shirt.

A month ago, being protected by a man that carried a firearm would have seemed strange and worrisome to her. Now, she accepted it as a normal part of life and what it took to survive.

"How's your dad?" Gen asked. She hadn't seen Liam Cuttaham since Atticus came for her at the ranch. Mark and her grandfather had saved her, and it was then that she found out her grandfather was alive and the famed Merlin.

"He's good. Had to take a long-overdue leave."

Gen nodded. She had found out later that Liam had been dying at St. Philip's Memorial hospital and was one of the patients miraculously healed when she brought Mark back from the dead.

"I need your help, Theo."

She saw him relax but still wondered what could have him so worked up.

"What do you need, Gen?"

Mark studied Theo silently.

He noticed Theo's unease the moment he saw him and wondered if they had walked into a trap. The accursed immortals had taught Mark that anything was possible, so he was prepared for anything.

He used his new ability to quickly scan Theo for any form of magic. Ever since he came back from the dead, Mark had been able to see and perceive magic. What looked like a mist swirled around Theo and pulsated with his heartbeat.

Over the days since, he had trained himself quietly, learning how to turn the power on and off. When he walked into the sheriff's office with Gen, he had switched it on.

Theo was afraid. Mark didn't know what had him so scared that he could sense the thumping of his heart from such a distance, but he had an idea. So, Mark watched and waited.

Gen leaned against one of the desks. Theo hadn't offered her a seat, and she wasn't going to ask.

"I need someone's picture drawn."

Theo frowned. She knew he would be curious, but she didn't want to drag him into her world. It was safer for him if he didn't know what was going on.

"Something happened, and I need to find someone. I don't know where or who they are, but I remember his face."

"You were attacked?" Theo turned to Mark in a fury.

"No, no. Nothing like that. I…I need to find someone, and I thought you could help us with a sketch artist."

Mark hadn't moved from his position by the wall. A lazy grin tugged the corner of his mouth, looking like an adult watching kids playing.

Damn the man!

Coming to Theo had been the only move they could make. She didn't know anybody else who could help, and Mark said that his connections could only track known individuals.

"What are you not saying, Gen? You never did explain why that government agent was after you. And why does Mr. Reynolds follow you everywhere you go?"

Theo tugged at the collar of his uniform. He tried to avoid looking in Mark's direction.

"Theo, I know you want answers, but could you trust me? I'm on a very important assignment."

"You work for the government too? Are you like, a secret agent?"

"Something like that. But I don't work for the government." Gen glanced at Mark, pleading for help. Mark looked at her and shook his head, the smile never leaving his lips.

Technically, she wasn't lying. She worked for a power higher than the Canadian government.

"Can you help me, Theo? I'll explain everything; answer any question when this is over."

A look of uncertainty filled his face. Gen almost felt sorry for him. He was like an open book, and that was another reason she couldn't bring herself to tell him anything. He wasn't the type who could keep secrets.

Theo sighed. She knew he would help her.

"We don't have what you need here in Dundurn, but there's a sketch artist at Saskatoon Police Service. I could make some calls, but I don't think they'll be so willing to allow your whole cloak and dagger stuff to slide. They'll need some concrete reason to get their sketch artist for you."

Gen looked at Mark. This was getting above her expertise. She was a student of business administration, not James Bond.

Mark walked over to Theo.

"Make your call. Let them know that you're bringing a witness to a crime and need their sketch artist to help."

"And what crime would that be?" Theo snapped in irritation.

"Let them know that you may have a lead on the assault on Sheriff Cuttaham."

Theo's head snapped back at Mark. His hand moved slowly to his hip holster as he stared into the piercing grey eyes of the man towering before him.

Theo knew they knew something about the night his father was attacked at Gen's ranch. He wondered if Mark had a hand in hurting him.

The air around them changed. He had experienced this same pressure when Agent Clarke came looking for Gen.

Mark didn't move, but Theo felt fear creep up his spine, and the little office suddenly felt hot and stifling. The animalistic part of his nature screamed at him to flee. It could sense the presence of an apex predator, and Theo knew he wouldn't remain standing if he drew his gun.

He felt a hand on his shoulder, and the moment passed. He looked to see Gen staring at him, pleading for help with her touch.

"We aren't the enemy here, Theo. You know that. Help us stop people from hurting others."

He found himself nodding, realizing for the first time that Gen was wearing sunglasses and that he had been seeing his own reflection all the while.

Lucilius felt empty.

A gaping hole resided where his beating heart should be, and he knew the reason why. He had long felt the soothing presence of the nail in their midst, and now it was gone.

Not stolen—that he could understand and live with. Humans were cunning and getting hood-winked would have been painful, but bearable.

No, the nail had been handed over. A willful transfer that had left him bitter and angry yet powerless to do anything about it.

Lucilius hated being powerless.

He looked around the bar and gulped down a shot of whisky. It was his fourth shot, but he didn't feel the buzz that came with drunkenness. He couldn't get drunk. He couldn't even remember the last time he was tipsy.

A couple at an adjacent table looked at him with something approaching disdain or pity, and his anger boiled.

What right did they have to gaze at him that way? They should be on their knees, begging for mercy. He was immortal, a god among men; they needed to respect that.

He had walked the earth long before the thought to conceive their lineage was formed. He may be dressed like them in blue denim jeans and a plain white shirt, but he wasn't like them.

The couple must have felt his anger because they hastily got to their feet and walked out of the bar.

Remus walked in as they left. He stood by the door, scanning the room, and Lucilius raised his hand to beckon him over.

"So, how did it go?" he asked when Remus sat beside him.

"He asked after you."

Lucilius grunted. He was angry, but he wasn't suicidal. He would have been crushed like an ant under a heel if he had shown his anger to their boss and master.

No, better not to turn up than accept a fate worse than death.

"What did he want?"

Remus pulled out a sheet of paper and slid it across the table.

"He wants these people taken out."

Lucilius felt his anger rise again. He knew this was a form of punishment for botching the last job, but it didn't stop him resenting it.

"Is this what we've become? Petty killers sent to do his bidding? Any one of his men could handle that." He started crumbling the paper, but Remus put a hand on his arm to restrain him.

"This is a chance to get back into his good graces, Lucilius. I don't know about you, but I'm willing to do whatever he says."

That was Remus's way. He was immortal but still a coward, unwilling to put himself in any form of danger. He realized suddenly that he had come into the bar with his own face. Remus could shapeshift, and he had taken on so many faces over the years that Lucilius had almost forgotten what the real one looked like.

He was a slim man with a neatly trimmed goatee. Lucilius couldn't tell if he used his ability to keep the beard evenly shaped or if he used scissors or a blade.

He scanned the names on the paper. Four had addresses next to them, and the name at the top belonged to a person who lived in Saskatoon.

"This will be quick," Lucilius said as he handed the paper back to Remus.

"We start at the top?" Remus asked, shoving it in his pocket.

Lucilius shrugged. It didn't matter to him either way.

Dead was dead.

Theo made the call to Saskatoon Police Service and secured an appointment with Sergeant Oliver Barbeau. Gen tried making small talk after that, but Theo remained uncharacteristically quiet, answering only yes or no. She was sad to see Theo drifting away from her. She valued their friendship, thinking of him like a brother, even though she knew he had always liked her.

"You know you could have been more helpful back there," she said, elbowing Mark as they left.

"You were doing well, and I didn't want to disturb you."

"Why antagonize him like that?"

Mark shrugged. "Wasn't trying to rile him, but knowing how security forces work, I thought we'd get more cooperation from them if it concerned one of their own."

"I still think that was a low blow."

Mark shrugged again. He had a better understanding of how these things worked, and though he knew it wouldn't get him any points with Theo, he knew bringing up his father's incident would be effective.

Mark surveyed the area as they walked to the car. Dundurn wasn't a threat, but given what he had seen since arriving, he wouldn't be surprised if a portal opened up and bad guys swarmed out in droves. He watched as a young mum holding the hand of a limping girl as they walked, then turned around and noticed Gen wasn't by his side anymore.

"Hi, Derby," Gen said, walking over. The woman smiled and said hello. They had never really socialized, but Dundurn being Dundurn, everybody's personal life was like an open book.

"What's wrong, Ava?" Gen asked, bending down to the little girl.

"Her leg's acting up again," Derby said. "We're off to see Harper. Maybe he'll have something for the pain before we head out to Saskatoon."

Gen knew about Ava. She had an accident when she was a baby that affected the growth of her left leg. The ankle had grown twisted and caused her to limp. The little girl's grimace of pain made Gen wish she could—

The world split before her eyes. She felt herself being pulled into a whirling vortex and reappearing in another world.

She was having another vision, but this time, it was different.

"What's wrong with you?" Ava's voice was muffled and distant. Gen saw herself splitting into two.

She could still see herself squatting beside Ava on the dusty, Dundurn road, but at the same time, she was elsewhere.

Gen looked around. Again, she was in the midst of a large crowd, but unlike before, she was outdoors. People pressed and jostled one another as they formed a small circle around a man Gen knew was Jesus Christ of Nazareth.

She realized her eyesight was normal, and she could see the gentle look of compassion on Jesus's face. The power emanating from Jesus gave her a sense of warmth and love.

Jesus looked around the mass of people. "Who touched me?" He asked.

Those close beside Him looked around, and then one spoke.

"Master, a large crowd is pressing against us, and we are being pushed from every corner. People have been touching you for a while now."

"Simon Peter, I can feel that spiritual power has gone out of me. Someone has touched me."

Gen noticed a woman standing at the edge of the crowd nearest to Jesus. She had her head bowed and was trembling.

"It was I," the woman whispered, but no one other than Gen heard her. Gen watched as she summoned her courage and stepped out of the safety of the crowd.

"It was I, Master," the woman repeated and fell on her knees before Jesus.

"I touched you because I believed you could heal me from my blood affliction of twelve years. As I saw you passing, I told myself that if I could touch the hem of your robe, I would be healed, and I was healed."

A hush settled over the crowd, and Simon Peter looked first at the woman and then at Jesus in amazement. He bent down and gently pulled the woman to her feet.

"Be of good cheer, daughter of Zion. Your faith in me has healed you and made you whole. Go in peace and remain whole."

Gen noticed one of the men closest to Jesus was dressed in rich apparel and had a guard by his side. There was a commotion as a group of guards shoved the people aside, and one of the guards came to the richly-dressed man and bowed.

"You mustn't trouble the Master. Your daughter has passed on."

"No!" the rich man lamented.

Jesus turned to the man and said, "Don't be afraid, Jairus. Have faith, and your daughter will be made whole."

Jesus walked on with Jairus, and the crowd followed. Gen remained still, processing what she had witnessed.

A concept nagged at the corner of her mind. She knew love and compassion made her able to bring Mark back from the dead, but this felt different.

It seemed faith and belief played a big role—faith in God and belief in His power.

The vision faded, and Gen saw that she was still beside Ava.

The visions were always purposeful. They were what they were for a reason.

She remembered the one she had weeks ago. It seemed like a lifetime had passed since, but she remembered the words clearly.

Gen looked at Ava with her new eyes and saw that her body radiated full health. Ava's light shone bright, and the little girl stood without any impediment. This was the Ava that Gen saw, and she was moved with compassion.

She rested her hand on Ava's head and allowed her desire for Ava to be healed to spring out.

"Be made whole," Gen whispered. A desire to see Ava in the same way she saw her soul, her bright light, filled her.

She felt power flow from her inner being and down her arm. Her spiritual sight made it possible to watch as the power entered Ava and rushed to her damaged ankle.

The girl gasped and looked at her mother.

"Mum, I don't feel the pain anymore."

Derby looked confused as Ava wiggled her foot.

Gen's heart almost burst when she saw Ava smile for the first time without pain. She ran around her mum, laughing and repeating, "Mum, the pain is gone!"

Derby turned tear-filled eyes to Gen and grabbed her hands in gratitude.

"I don't know what you did or how you did it but thank you, thank you so much." Gen nodded and looked around. They were attracting a crowd. Mark must have sensed the need to extract her because he appeared from nowhere and guided her quickly to the car.

"What was that?" Mark asked as they drove back to the ranch.

"I don't know. I had a vision and saw Jesus healing a woman."

"And you decided it was a good idea to replicate the act?"

"What? No, Ava's been in pain for years. She's such a brave kid. She tries to hide it from her mother, but I could feel the depth of her pain. Some days are worse than others, Mark. I couldn't leave her like that."

"I'm not judging, Gen. Just wondering about the attention this will bring."

Gen was silent. She'd been restless for the past two weeks, and she felt this was the direction she needed to head in.

"We'll deal with that when we have to," Mark nodded.

Josephine sat watching a sitcom with her feet curled beneath her like a cat, a bowl of popcorn and a half-empty soda bottle at her side. She had been sick for so long that she just needed some time to herself. Her aunt had understood and hadn't said anything.

Josephine knew she couldn't continue this way. She was back with the living and had to join the endless throng of humanity struggling to make ends meet.

She wondered if she could get her former job back. The school administrator had been understanding when the pain made it impossible to teach and said space would always be available for her.

She imagined the look on his face if she showed up now; they hadn't expected her to survive.

She hadn't expected to survive either, so she probably couldn't blame them.

Like her aunt always said, life goes on.

3

ergeant Oliver Barbeau turned out to be a short, squat man with puffy red cheeks. He was all-business and directed Mark and Gen to an interrogation room without conversation, where they sat and waited for the sketch artist.

Mark pulled out one of the two chairs for Gen, then ambled around the table in the centre of the room. He peered into the two-way mirror covering half of one of the walls and extended his essence.

They were alone.

After a few minutes, a young man in glasses walked in, holding a tablet and a stylus. He introduced himself as he sat across from Gen, but Mark didn't bother remembering the name. They wouldn't meet after today, anyway.

Mark stood at the back of the room while Gen described the images from her visions and let his mind wander as he watched over the "bearer of the foot nail."

That's what Lucilius and the others had called her: Nail Bearer. A title covering a long lineage of women given the charge of protecting the nails used to crucify Jesus Christ.

Mark had seen a lot of amazing things since agreeing to watch over her. One immortal wielding lightning like a pencil, another shooting an unending supply of magic arrows from God knows where. Lucilius, the sword-fighting immortal who could cut a bullet in two.

Mark was nudged back to the room when he noticed the sketch artist standing and shaking Gen's hand. As he left the room, Gen turned to Mark.

"So, what's next?"

"I don't think they'll give us any information if they get a hit. They'll probably send it to Theo, so we might need to get to Mr. Cuttaham to get any answers."

"What if we ask Sergeant Barbeau nicely?"

"I don't think your charms will work on Sergeant Barbeau. Looks like the by-the-book kind of guy."

"I can be very persuasive," Gen teased lightly.

Mark smiled and leaned back on the seat. He knew Gen had been pushing herself since the incident two weeks ago. Somehow, she blamed herself for Lucilius's attack. He was glad to see her take things lightly for a change.

They heard footsteps approaching, and Sergeant Barbeau entered the room.

"We've got a match. Two, actually. But it seems your intel may be incorrect. One's a teacher, and the other's a doctor. Both with clean records, and one of them has been in the hospital for cancer treatment. How can they be involved in the attack on Sheriff Cuttaham?"

The sergeant eyed Gen and then Mark. He didn't mention that he'd run checks on both of them, too. While they had clean records, the fact that Mark was ex-military was suspicious. And he could tell there was some kind of chemistry between them, even though Mark was obviously much older than Gen.

Mark knew he had to come up with something believable, or they'd become suspects number one and two themselves. He had seen the glances Sergeant Barbeau had given him and, if the roles had been reversed, he would probably do a background check too.

Mark hoped that would be enough to get them out of the present predicament.

"Unfortunately, Sergeant, we aren't at liberty to tell you anything more at the moment. There is more to this case than just the assault on Sheriff Cuttaham," Mark said.

"And what would that be?"

Mark shrugged his shoulders, indicating that he wasn't in a position to reveal any secrets to Sergeant Barbeau. He gestured for Gen to stand, then stretched out his hand. Sergeant Barbeau reluctantly gripped it in a firm handshake.

"Thanks a lot for the assistance. You've been a big help, and we'll let the higher-ups know of your cooperation."

Mark guided Gen out of the room with a protective hand on her back and headed for the exit. They needed to get out before Sergeant Barbeau decided to hold them while making calls to ascertain their credentials.

They reached the car park without being stopped, and Mark released a big sigh of relief. "That was close."

Gen nodded as she shut the door, and Mark started the car.

"Thought we were heading for jail. Can't believe he let us go," Gen said.

"Where to?"

"Home. We'll meet up with Theo and find out what he was sent."

Gen leaned back in the car seat and shut her eyes. For a moment back there, she had thought things would turn violent, and she knew Mark would have done anything to protect her. Unlike her grandfather, Mark's skills rested more with the physical aspects of combat. He was a skilled warrior, and she wasn't afraid for him as much as of what he could do. He had tangled with magicians and sword experts and come out standing. That changed people, and she knew he was no exception.

How much change was yet to be seen, though.

They drove in silence when Gen felt a pull tugging at her spirit.

"Stop the car, Mark," she spoke urgently.

Mark reacted swiftly and swerved to the curb; at the same time, he reached into his jacket pocket.

Gen's eyes widened in surprise when she saw the gun in his hand. She hadn't seen him draw it.

Mark ignored the honking of car horns from angry drivers. "What's wrong?" he asked, scanning the area around their car.

Gen had recognized the feeling tugging at her spirit. "I can sense another nail, Mark."

He glanced at her questioningly, and she nodded. "I'm sure. The same feeling as the last time."

Mark nodded, not questioning further. He had long ago agreed that when it came to matters of visions, nails, and the supernatural, Gen was the expert.

"Do you have an exact location?"

"No, but it's close. Not too close, but it's here in Saskatoon."

"Then let's head home. Myrddin should hear this as well."

Gen nodded. Her grandfather needed to know about the nail. He was more informed than they were when it came to this. Mark turned and joined the traffic, and they headed back to Dundurn.

Myrddin took the coffee Mark handed him and turned to Gen. From where they sat in the kitchen, Mark realized he could see a large oak tree through the window.

"You say you felt the presence of another nail?" Myrddin asked.

"Yes, on our way back from the police station in Saskatoon. Theo connected us to a sergeant there.

The feeling was faint, as though very distant or covered somehow."

"They must be using a cloaking spell to keep the power muted. You shouldn't be able to sense anything, though," Myrddin frowned. Things were going a lot faster than he had hoped. His plan had been to guide her into the role she was meant to play gradually, but the situation kept changing. The accursed had struck sooner than he expected, and he had to change plans to adapt.

He couldn't recall any of the other nail bearers being able to sense a nail without another one's presence. Then there were the visions.

From the accounts he received from Empress Helena, physical contact with the nail was the only sure way of activating a vision, but it seemed Gen didn't need it.

"It could be a trap," Mark mentioned.

Myrddin looked up from his mug. The thought had occurred to him, too. It could be the work of Lucilius and Remus, the remaining immortals who were after the nails.

"We can't be sure about that," Gen objected.

"But we don't know anything for sure. This looks like their game book. Lure us with the scent of one of the nails and attack us at a place of their choosing."

"Mark, we can't ignore this."

"Don't get me wrong, Gen; I agree that we have to do something. But we need more intel and maybe a plan of our own. We don't know if it's the nail with them or the third nail we've been looking for."

Myrddin placed his cup on the kitchen table. "You both have valid points. We can't ignore this, but we can also assume it's a trap and plan accordingly."

"I propose Myrddin and I go check out the location," Mark said firmly.

Myrddin winced at his protective gesture and, knowing his granddaughter, he wasn't surprised when Gen glared at Mark.

"I refuse to be benched again. I can take care of myself. I've been doing that most of my life."

"Now, now, Gen. You know Mark means well, and he does have a point."

Myrddin patted Gen's hand. He could see that Mark looked hurt by Gen's outburst. Gen must have realized it, too, because she took a deep breath and turned to Mark.

"Sorry about that. It's just…I know something's about to go down, but I can't place my finger on what. It's very frustrating, and I'm sorry for taking it out on you."

Mark nodded, and Myrddin saw Gen's sigh of relief.

That's the thing with having feelings for someone: they're the ones who can hurt you the most. But they're also the ones who can love you the most.

Gen's phone rang, and Myrddin was glad for the distraction.

"Hello? Hey, Theo…yeah? Okay…thanks." Gen hung up and explained Theo wanted her to check her email, where he had sent the addresses of the teacher and the doctor.

"They both live in Saskatoon. The teacher is staying at Blairmore and the doctor at Fairhaven. What do we do?"

"What if we all go to Saskatoon and meet these people?" Mark offered.

"What about the nail?"

"We can get to that after we find these two."

Myrddin watched Gen and Mark go back and forth and mulled over the options.

"We don't know how long the nail will remain in one place."

"If it's a trap, Gen, I don't think they'll be in a hurry to leave."

"But what if it isn't a trap?"

It was a circular argument, and Myrddin cleared his throat to get their attention.

"It's obvious we have to split up and—" he raised his hand to stop Mark from protesting, "And while it's not such a great idea, we have to. Gen is the only one here who can sense the nail, so the real question is who follows her and who goes to Blairmore?"

There was silence as the three of them tried to figure out the best option. Mark watched Gen fidgeting with her earlobe while Myrddin remained quiet, waiting for Gen and Mark to agree on a course of action.

"I still don't see why we can't all go and check the nail and then get to Blairmore," Mark said.

Gen wanted to agree, but she couldn't shake the feeling that they needed to hurry. "I don't know how to say this, but I have a feeling that we need to get to them quickly."

"What do you mean?"

"I can't explain it, but I have a feeling of danger whenever I think of the seven."

Mark pinched the bridge of his nose and sighed. He had learnt not to disregard Gen's hunches; she could tap into the supernatural and seemed to have a keen sense of when trouble was brewing.

"Okay, Gen. You and Myrddin check out the nail. I'll head over to Saskatoon and check on the addresses."

Mark could see the look of relief on Gen's face as he got to his feet. He reached the door when Gen called his name.

"Go to the teacher first," she said.

Mark raised an eyebrow at that.

"I can't explain that either, but I kind of have this feeling that she's in greater danger. And be careful."

"Always."

Mark's gaze locked on Myrddin, and an unspoken communication passed between the two of them. Myrddin nodded his head in understanding, and Mark felt some of the tension leave his shoulders.

Mark headed to the barn to prepare.

Finding Josephine Braddock's address was as simple as searching her name on Google. The top result was a link to her Facebook, and there was Josephine's life—open for all to see.

Isabella scrolled through her page and, from the information there, learned that Josephine was, or rather, had been a teacher before her cancer worsened. Her last update was weeks ago, more of a farewell note to her pupils and friends. If she really had been miraculously healed of cancer, Isabella smelt the making of a scoop.

She steered her car onto the curb and switched off the engine. Before moving, she paused to look at the building across the road, trying to get her head into the game.

She needed this.

It was her chance to enter the big leagues. She would be world-famous; she could imagine herself reporting the biggest stories and her face on huge billboards.

Her first hurdle came when she stopped in front of the building. It had numerous identical apartments and knowing which one was Josephine's looked impossible.

She pressed a random bell and waited for a response.

"Who is it?" a gruff voice asked.

"Delivery service."

There was a moment of silence, and Isabella held her breath. Then a click sounded, and the door slid open.

Isabella tried not to pump her fist as she entered the building.

First obstacle crossed. Now she needed to find Josephine's apartment. Isabella did what any aspiring reporter would—she knocked on the first door that caught her fancy.

On her third attempt, the door creaked open a couple of inches and a little girl standing peered out from behind it.

"Hello. Does Josephine Baddock live here?"

The girl pointed to the door opposite, and Isabella waved and thanked her.

What if Josephine wasn't home? She hadn't considered that possibility.

She knocked, then knocked again, and was about to try a final time when she heard the lock turn.

Josephine now bore little resemblance to the pictures of herself online. Isabella might not have recognized her if not for her striking blue eyes; the woman who stood before her was gaunt and looked at least ten years older. She had a buzz cut, and Isabella couldn't tell if it was a fashion statement or a result of chemo.

"Hello, my name is Isabella from the *Daily Sun*. If you don't mind, I'd like to ask you a few questions."

Josephine looked her up and down, then shrugged and walked back into the apartment, leaving the door open behind her. Isabella hesitated before following. By the time she entered, Josephine was already sitting on the sofa with her feet curled underneath her.

Isabella sat on the opposite chair.

"What do you want?"

Isabella looked around, hoping for a clue about how to approach this. The apartment was clean and neat but sparsely decorated; there was nothing to indicate its occupant's personality or state of mind. Isabella decided to try a different approach from her usual openers.

"How did it feel?"

Josephine blinked and cocked her head slightly. Isabella smiled, hoping to put her at ease.

"How did what feel?"

"The moment you got healed, how did it feel? Did you feel your body change?" She had hundreds of questions, but she needed to take it slowly, so she resisted her excited urge to push and waited in silence as Josephine collected her thoughts.

"Have you ever experienced pain so severe that it knocked you unconscious? An endless agony that washes away every other feeling? I knew I was dying. I didn't just accept it; I welcomed it. Death meant the torture would end. One moment I was swimming in pain, and the next, it was gone."

Josephine took a deep breath. She hadn't once looked up from her trembling hands, and she kept her gaze on them as she began speaking again.

"There wasn't a gradual easing of the pain. It didn't reduce in degree. I was overwhelmed one second, and then it was gone. For the first time in over a year, I could take a deep breath without tears stinging my eyes. That's what happened to me. I don't know what you'd call that, but it was real."

An uncomfortable silence settled in the room. Isabella didn't know what she had expected, but it wasn't this.

She could feel the depth of emotion in Josephine's words. That she had experienced healing couldn't be denied. She nodded slowly, wondering how she could turn this tale to suit her needs.

Though Mark had been reluctant to allow Gen to go without him, he understood her reasoning. Even from a distance, he knew her intuition could guide him, so, as she advised, he drove to the teacher's address first.

He came prepared. He never went anywhere without his Glock .45 and, not knowing what he might be about to walk into, he had also strapped a recurve blade to his wrist and packed a canvas bag. It sat on the floorboard of the front passenger seat, containing an MP7, flash grenades, and night-vision goggles. He had thought about bringing his sword but decided against it; it would be too conspicuous.

Mark parked on the curb a few meters from an imposing, brutalist-style building. Josephine Baddock lived here in Apartment 6 with her aunt, who had taken her in when the cancer made it impossible for her to live alone.

He crossed the street, looking both ways and checking for exit points, a force of habit he had no intention of changing. At the front door, he pressed the bell next to the hand-scrawled number 6.

"Who's this?" a feminine voice asked.

"Hello, I'm from St. Philip's Memorial Hospital…"

"I told you guys I'm done with tests. I'm not going back there."

"That's why I'm here. I need your confirmation signature on our release form."

"I signed that at the hospital."

"Yes, you did, but this is a follow-up. It's a requirement. After this, we'll be out of your hair."

The door buzzed open.

Theo hated not knowing what was going on. When his father kept him out of the loop, he had found him virtually dead at Gen's ranch. That wouldn't happen again; he wouldn't allow it.

Gen was hiding something. It had bothered him all day, along with the memory of Mark breathing down his neck. There was something off about them. Why was she wearing dark sunglasses in the office? Was Mark hurting her?

He looked capable enough and exuded an air of barely restrained violence.

Could Gen be hiding bruises underneath those glasses?

Surely she would tell him if she were in an abusive relationship, though? She must know Theo would protect her. But she had changed since she came back from university in Toronto.

She was so different; he had been willing to believe she was part of a terrorist group when he heard the accusation a few weeks ago. Even though he now realized it wasn't true, she was still hiding something from him.

His frustration grew as he looked at the addresses he had emailed her. He had to know.

Theo drummed his fingers on the steering wheel of the sheriff's van as he drove to Saskatoon.

Lucilius felt humiliated.

He sat in the back of a black Jeep with Remus by his side, by their master's orders, being driven by two men in the front. They were babysitters, and there was nothing Lucilius could do about it.

The list of individuals to kill didn't include any explanation about why they had to die, but that didn't bother him. He just seethed that their master didn't trust him anymore and sent goons to watch over him.

Once, he had been an agent for change, spreading death and disaster across continents for eons. He had ruled nations at the behest of his master, and now he was relegated to the bench, a discarded tool that wasn't sharp enough.

Well, he would prove his worth again. He would climb through bodies, dreams, and aspirations to reclaim his place of honour again.

Lucilius looked through the tinted window as they drove to the second target. The first, a doctor, hadn't returned from his shift, and while Remus could have infiltrated the hospital, Lucilius wanted the privilege of the first kill. He wanted to witness his victim's life slip away. Maybe that would appease the hunger in his black soul?

He needed to see pain and suffering.

4

Mark had seen a photo of Josephine on the printout Gen acquired from Theo, and he wasn't expecting the thin, frail woman before him.

"Josephine Baddock?" he asked.

She nodded but remained silent.

"May I come in? This will only take a moment."

Josephine opened the door wider, and Mark walked into her apartment, immediately noticing another woman there. She looked too young to be Josephine's aunt, and there didn't seem to be any family resemblance.

"Can I offer you anything?" Josephine asked. "Coffee?"

"No, thank you."

Mark had expected her to be alone and was a little taken aback by the stranger. He noticed she had a small tape recorder, the kind usually carried by journalists.

"The form?" Josephine asked, ready with a pen in her hand.

"About that …"

Mark had considered dressing as a police officer but was worried she might not agree to let him in.

"The form from the hospital?" she repeated, irritated.

"I don't think he's from the hospital," Isabella remarked. She was watching Mark closely. He had scanned the room carefully when he entered and carried himself with more precision than a hospital worker.

"What?" Josephine asked Isabella.

"Doesn't look like a hospital worker to me."

"Another reporter!" Josephine groaned.

She was tired of them hounding her; she wasn't even sure why she let Isabella into her home. One had snuck into her hospital room disguised as a cleaner; another pretended to be a long-lost relative. Now, this tall, handsome, sturdy individual had also come under false pretenses. She was still trying to get her mind around what had happened and just wanted to be left alone.

"I'm sorry for the pretense, but I wasn't sure you'd agree to see me," Mark hastily replied. Isabella frowned; he could tell she didn't believe he was a fellow practitioner of the noble art of journalism. It was time he came clean.

"I'm not a reporter either, Miss Josephine."

"I knew it!" Isabella blurted. He couldn't be; he screamed military or something in that field.

"Who are you?" Josephine asked warily. She couldn't understand what games the stranger was playing.

"My name is Mark Reynolds, and I'm in the security business. I'm here to tell you that your life is in danger."

He watched their expressions keenly. Josephine looked confused and wary, but the reporter's eyes widened to epic proportions.

Again, he pondered how best to explain the situation and decided that the truth was the best approach.

"What are you talking about?" the reporter asked, but Mark ignored her and looked at Josephine. He could sense her fear.

"What do you want?" It was almost a whisper.

"Look, I'm not here to hurt you, and what I'm saying is the truth. You are in danger."

"From whom?" Isabella asked, moving to Josephine's side. He nodded internally in approval. Though the two women wouldn't stand a chance against him. If he really was here to attack them, sticking together was their only option to increase their odds of survival.

Josephine looked from Mark to Isabella. He knew that she would soon attempt to escape if he couldn't reach her.

"Please, calm down. Like I said, I'm not here to harm you. I was in St. Philip's Memorial Hospital two weeks ago. Like you, I wasn't in the best of health, but unlike you, I died."

"You what? Are you nuts?" Until this point, Isabella had been trying to figure out Mark's angle, but now she wondered if he belonged in a psych ward.

Isabella couldn't believe her luck. This was the beginning of a life-changing story, and the hunk standing before her was the key. He had the look of someone dangerous but, since she was still alive, she would trust her gut feeling that she was safe in his presence.

She noticed his words seemed to resonate with Josephine; she looked less like a field mouse about to be caught by a hawk. The best part was that she still had her mini-recorder on, and it was capturing every word.

"What are you saying?" Josephine asked.

"I'm guessing here, but I believe you were gravely ill, you saw a flash of white light, and suddenly, you were healed," Mark explained.

Josephine stopped herself from nodding, but he could tell he was right. He followed the news closely during that period, and every patient interviewed told the same story.

Unfortunately, the press reported a skewed version of what really happened and scoffed at the notion of a ward full of people being simultaneously and miraculously healed. They came up with all sorts of hypotheses and explanations until no one was interested in the story at all.

But the people directly involved knew.

Mark was patient zero at ground zero; the healing began with him. He lay dead on a theatre table in the hospital, succumbing to a sword fatally thrust into his heart, and Gen had resurrected him. She explained that a bright light exploded from her, which both healed and defended her against Atticus, the immortal mage who was there to kill her.

The light obliterated Atticus into nothing, and went on to heal every sick, injured, or infirm patient in the hospital. Everyone felt its force, even the hospital's staff, and while some had believed, others were skeptical and called the phenomenon a coincidence.

"But how does all this put me in danger?"

"I can't exactly say, but I believe your life is in danger because of that occurrence."

"Okay, let me get this straight. She got healed, and now she's in danger because of it? You almost had me going there," Isabella snorted in disbelief. Maybe she was right the first time; there was no story. This man must be crazy or confused; even if he did have eyes you could drown in—and probably die happy, too.

Mark sighed. Isabella's reaction made him realize how crazy he must sound from her perspective.

But what else could he say? He was here because he believed in Gen and believed in her visions. Josephine Baddock was important somehow, and it was up to him to convince her that she needed his help.

The sudden buzz of the doorbell made the two women jump. Mark spun around, then nodded when Josephine looked at him, unsure if her questioning eyes were seeking permission or assurance. She walked to the intercom and pressed the button.

"Yes?"

"Josephine Baddock?"

"Yes."

"Delivery for you."

"Are you expecting anything?" Mark whispered.

"Don't think so. My aunt may be, though," she mouthed back.

Mark put a firm but calm hand on her arm to stop her from pushing the button that would open the building's door.

"Tell him you're not expecting anything."

"Why?"

"Because you aren't expecting a delivery. It's unwise to open the door to strangers."

Josephine raised an eyebrow and looked from Mark to Isabella.

"You shouldn't have let us in, either," Mark added.

The doorbell buzzed again.

"Sorry, I'm not expecting any delivery."

The situation could be one of two things: either there really was a delivery, in which case, the man at the door would continue to argue, or, the other option, danger was at her door.

The silence that followed was his answer. Trouble had arrived. Gen was right.

Lucilius leaned against the building's brick wall as the first henchman pressed the bell for a different apartment. Josephine Baddock hadn't fallen for their ruse, but they weren't giving up. If they had to, he would kick the door down and slaughter everyone inside.

He had done it before. Better to complete the mission, even if that meant collateral damage.

Henchman One introduced himself as a delivery guy again, and the door clicked open.

Now for the fun part.

They needed to get out of the building immediately.

"Listen to me, Miss Baddock," Mark said sternly. He didn't want her to panic, but he needed her to listen. "The danger I talked about is here. You have to trust me—for your own good."

"Why should we do that?" Isabella asked. So, Josephine wasn't expecting a delivery, she thought. That was hardly grounds to turn this into an episode of *Mission Impossible*, even if this man could play the lead comfortably.

"Because if I'm right, we have a couple of minutes before this apartment becomes a battlefield. They know you are here, and they're coming for you. We need to move now."

"I don't understand. Why would anybody want me dead?"

Mark didn't have the answer, either. He was just following Gen's lead; he didn't know why Josephine needed to die. Maybe it wasn't because she had been healed, he wondered. Maybe she was part of the bigger picture, somehow a component in Gen's victory over the coming darkness. If that was true, then the enemy at her door was...

Mark swore.

He pulled out his Glock .45, and the two women screamed. It was the accursed. They were the ones after Josephine and the doctor.

"Get back. Into the bedroom, now, and don't come out. Is there any other exit?" He gripped Josephine's arm to get her attention away from the gun. "I'm here to protect you. Is there another way out of here?"

Josephine shook her head.

"Okay, get to the bedroom and find somewhere safe to hide."

Josephine nodded and bolted out of the sitting room. Isabella stood her ground; she would see this through to the end.

Mark appreciated the brave front the reporter was trying to put on, but she would only be a hindrance to the coming fight.

"Unless you want to be collateral damage, I'd advise you to follow Josephine and hide."

That broke her uncertainty. She dashed out of the room after Josephine.

Mark moved swiftly to the nearest wall and waited for the show to start.

Gen could still feel the nail, and the pull was getting stronger as they drove. She could tell she was changing, getting stronger in her spirit. What the final result would be, she didn't know. She didn't need the first nail anymore, so they had left it at the Triple 7 ranch, safe under her grandfather's unbreakable spell.

"It's getting stronger in that direction. You need to take the next right," she told him, wondering what could be going through his mind.

"Do you think it's a trap?" she asked.

"We'll know soon enough. I know you want to help, but you'll have to listen to me, Gen."

"Don't I?"

"Do you?" Myrddin countered with a chuckle.

Gen was strong. Her life force blazed brightly, but she lacked experience. Coupled with her stubborn streak, she could get into situations above her head quickly.

"Missing Mark?" Myrddin asked to change the subject. He could see her preparing to deny it, but she folded her arms instead.

"It's that obvious?"

"I'm an old man. Not much gets by me. And yes, it's pretty obvious to anyone who can see. So, take it from someone who has seen a couple of lifetimes; enjoy your time with those you love and who love you, too. Life can sometimes be very fleeting."

Gen looked at her grandfather. She wondered who he had lost during the millennia he had walked the earth. She patted his hand on the steering wheel and nodded, an understanding passing between them, and Myrddin smiled.

Suddenly, she looked up and pointed. "There! The nail is there."

Myrddin steered the truck to a crawl and parked. He extended his spiritual senses, and the building facing them lit up like a carnival.

He wondered what else might be waiting for them inside.

Mark flattened himself against the wall when he heard a whirling sound. Seconds later, there was a muffled thud, and the apartment door swung in slowly.

He groaned internally. This had the markings of professionals, and he wasn't surprised when a flash grenade rolled into the sitting room.

He covered his face to protect it from the flash that lit the room like lightning in the night sky, but he still waited, even as he heard footsteps pound into the room. The muzzle of a gun appeared, and an arm followed. Mark allowed the first assailant to go past him before he moved.

He slammed his gun against the man's head, but he reacted swiftly, dodging the blow and rolling away, leaving Mark exposed for the second assailant to take him down.

At least, that was their plan.

Mark twisted, his recurve blade flashing in the air as it spun and embedded in the second assailant's flesh. He tracked the first assailant as he rose to his feet and pulled the gun's trigger twice. The first assailant staggered forward and fell to the ground.

He then advanced to the second, who was struggling to pull the blade from his chest, when Mark heard someone clapping.

"Well done, Protector. Well done."

He recognized the voice instantly, and rage welled up in him as Lucilius and Remus strode into the apartment.

Gen and Myrddin walked into what looked like an empty warehouse.

"I can still sense the nail. It's here." Gen was confused. The pull was strong here, but she couldn't see anything, even with her spiritual senses. The warehouse felt as empty as it looked.

"What's going on, Granddad?"

Myrddin grunted. The nail was here and yet not here. A cloaking spell was hiding the nail, and he was surprised he couldn't seem to break it.

What spell could be strong enough that he couldn't pierce the veil?

He felt his heart beat faster as something he hadn't felt in eons slid down his spine.

Myrddin was afraid.

Isabella wished she had a camera instead of the voice recorder she held in her shaking hand.

She couldn't believe her eyes. She had never seen anyone move so fast. Mark had taken down the two

73

assailants in seconds. She watched as he aimed his gun at the newcomers and again wished she had a camera.

Mark stared at Lucilius and Remus. The first assailant groaned and struggled to his feet.

"Are these like you two?" Mark asked.

One thing he remembered about the accursed was that they liked to talk. He would get them talking while he tried to think of an exit strategy that didn't involve dying.

"There are none like us," Lucilius boasted.

Mark was glad to hear that, and he aimed at the first assailant and pulled the trigger again. The force of the bullet threw the man to the ground again. For a second, Mark had considered going for a headshot, but he changed his mind. He was sure the two assailants would be wearing bulletproof vests under their custom-made black suits, and the man's groan was confirmation.

The second assailant had managed to pull the blade out of his chest but was breathing raggedly. It must have nicked something vital.

"I'd get that checked at a hospital soon if I were you," Mark told him.

"Do you really need these two, Lucilius? You never seemed like the type who liked help. Now, if it were the shitbag beside you, I'd have expected an army load of backups." Mark was glad to see Remus grind his teeth in anger.

Lucilius moved fast. One moment he was beside Remus; the next, he had his hands around the first assailant's neck. A crack sounded as he snapped his neck and smiled at Mark.

Mark didn't wait. He offloaded his clip into Lucilius's body and watched as the bullets riddled him. Lucilius fell to his knees but was still alive, even though Mark was sure one bullet had penetrated his head.

Has Lucilius grown stronger?

The air around Remus's fingertips shimmered, and Mark dived to the left, avoiding an arrow whisking past him and slamming into the opposite wall.

Mark heard a scream and cursed silently. Lucilius and Remus heard the sound, too.

Things were going to get very hairy now.

Mark knew they would try and divide his attention. One would remain to fight him while the other went for their target. With their powers and abilities, that plan would have worked against anybody. But Mark wasn't anybody.

He had fought Lucilius and Remus before and bested them. He didn't know what other tricks they had up their sleeves, but he wasn't the same anymore, either. He changed when he came back from the dead, and he had an ability he could count on. He could see and feel magic—the shimmer or displacement of air just before a spell was cast. He could also see the spiritual essence gather around an individual when the person planned to use magic.

And he saw the darkness spread across Lucilius's body, pushing out embedded bullets and healing him of critical wounds. Mark saw a tingling of tiny black spots as a portal opened before Remus's fingertips, and he plucked an arrow seemingly out of thin air.

He didn't wait. He pulled the trigger of his Glock and shot the arrow out of Remus's hand. Mark smiled when Remus screamed in pain. At the same time, he rushed at Lucilius.

Lucilius was a sword expert and had a super healing ability. Now was the time to find out how he fared in unarmed combat.

Mark drove his knee into Lucilius's chest, who blocked the move with his palm. From the corner of his eye, Mark saw Remus try to bring another arrow into this realm, so he shot Remus in the shoulder.

That should keep him out of the fight for a while.

Remus also healed from wounds, albeit much slower than Lucilius, and he was a coward. He would want to be in full health before engaging in the fight.

The distraction almost cost Mark his life as Lucilius drove his elbow at his face.

Well, that answered the question: Lucilius was an expert at unarmed combat.

He would have been defenceless against Lucilius's onslaught, but he had another edge: the memories of the first protector—the undisputed arena champion of the fourth century.

Mark turned his face to the side, and Lucilius's elbow swung past his face. They traded quick jabs too fast for the eyes to follow, but Mark relied on muscle memory. His palm slapped away a punch; he twisted his body to the side to avoid a powerful thrust that would have speared his floating ribs and punctured his lungs.

His knuckles crunched Lucilius's nose, but he got caught in a punch to a pressure point that numbed his right shoulder and made him unable to use his hand for some seconds.

He allowed himself to take a kick to the chest and used the momentum to roll away from Lucilius and take a breather.

Lucilius didn't follow. He straightened his bent nose to allow himself to breathe better. Mark felt the blood slowly circulating in his injured shoulder, and he clenched his right fist and waited.

He needed to end this quickly.

Myrddin prepared his teleportation spell as he turned to Gen.

"Something or someone is casting a veil over this place, and I can't break the spell." Myrddin looked at Gen. Even though her white eyes stared at him, he could tell she was troubled.

"You know what that means, Gen. I can't unravel the spell. We need to get out of here. Now."

Gen could sense the fear coursing through her grandfather's body.

What could make the greatest wizard in human history afraid? Gen wasn't sure she wanted to find out. She nodded for her grandfather to teleport them to safety.

The spell built around them, but Gen felt it fizzle to nothing.

"What's wrong, Granddad?"

Myrddin looked around. He scanned the warehouse for any object that could be emitting magic but found nothing.

"Something doesn't want us to leave." He shuffled through his mind for entities that could cast a containment shield this powerful.

A dragon had the power to cast a shield as powerful as this, but the time of dragons was over. A grand mage could cast a containment spell this strong, but Myrddin was sure he would have been able to break it eventually.

This radiated more power than he had felt since—

"Head for the exit, Gen. Now."

They had only taken a couple of steps when they felt a shimmering, and the containment barrier fell. Gen and Myrddin stumbled to a stop and looked around.

They were completely surrounded.

5

Mark was ready for round two.

Round two consisted of only one plan—a hasty retreat.

He hoped the apartment didn't really have only one exit. He moved backward slowly so as not to give away his intentions.

"How's the nose?" Mark asked.

"It will heal."

"Why are you here, Lucilius? There's no nail here. No nail bearer. What do you want the woman for?"

Lucilius didn't answer immediately, and Mark thought he would have to taunt him some more, but he finally replied. He took a step toward Mark and spread his arms wide open.

"I don't have any quarrel with the woman, Protector. She is just a name on a list."

A list? Why would the accursed have a hit list? It didn't make any sense. Mark watched Remus rotate his shoulder and crack his neck. Magic arrows would soon begin to fly, so Mark needed to finish the conversation and retreat.

"Why would you have a hit list? I thought you immortals weren't afraid of anyone. What has you so scared that you would take this cowardly route to kill your enemies? Where's the honour in that?" Mark spat the words at Lucilius. Lucilius had accused him of dishonour during their last fight, and Mark took pleasure in seeing the immortal squirm.

"They are not my enemies," Lucilius roared.

Mark had reached the short corridor leading to two bedrooms. He saw Isabella peeping through the door by his right and rushed that way. He pushed her gently into the bedroom and bolted it. Josephine hid in the corner of the room.

"Tell me you have another way out of here."

"There isn't," Josephine whimpered.

They heard a boom as the bedroom door shook. Mark rushed to the bathroom and saw a tiny window. "Over here, quickly." He pushed open the window and helped Josephine climb through.

"Your turn."

Isabella looked skeptically at the little hole.

"It's either that or those two back there."

Isabella didn't have to be told twice. She had seen Lucilius snap a man's neck like tiny twigs. She struggled through the small hole and almost had a bout of claustrophobia, but she was out before the terror could set in.

Mark heard the bedroom door give in as he struggled through the bathroom window. He landed on the fire exit and followed the two women down the stairs.

"This way." Mark said at the bottom, and the women hurriedly turned around and followed him toward his car. He yanked open the back door and pulled out his canvas bag. He swung the bag onto the hood of the car and unzipped it.

"What are you doing? Let's go," Isabella screamed at him.

"Get in," Mark commanded. He pulled out the MP7 and slammed a clip into it. "If it seems like things aren't going my way, get the hell out of here."

Mark turned to Josephine. "You need to get to Dundurn. Get to Triple 7 ranch. You will find safety there."

Josephine looked into Mark's eyes, then nodded.

He took an extra clip and went hunting, moving swiftly.

Lucilius and Remus would expect he would run away to safety, and he had every intention of doing that, but first, he needed to deliver a message.

If the accursed weren't after Josephine, it meant they were working for someone. Mark wanted their employer to know how costly it was to go against him. He reached the building's entrance just as Lucilius and Remus stepped out.

Mark aimed and pulled the trigger. Lucilius was fast, but Mark expected that. Lucilius wasn't his target. The bullets slammed into Remus's head, and he dropped like a sack of potatoes.

No more interfering magical arrows.

Lucilius tried to rush at Mark, but he wasn't bothered. They had done this dance too many times. Mark backstepped and aimed at Lucilius's legs. The bullets shattered his kneecaps, and he screamed as he collapsed in pain.

Lucilius and Remus may be immortals, but they felt pain like anyone else. Mark had thought of a way to neutralize their strength, and this was the best he had come up with—divide and conquer.

Remus was easy. The coward couldn't withstand pain and had a slower healing ability. Lucilius was the problem. He shrugged off bullet wounds like they were ant bites. Mark had spent some time researching the human body, looking for weaknesses that could be exploited and fragile areas that wouldn't heal quickly.

Lucilius moaned as he lay on the floor clutching one of his broken legs. Mark could only imagine the excruciating pain Lucilius was going through. Even growing the fragments of the kneecaps back would be painful.

Mark walked calmly up to him, cradling his MP7 in his arms.

"This is what it will cost you anytime you go against me or mine. You called me the Protector of the nail bearer, and that is what I am. Tell your boss that I know he exists now. I will find him, and I will kill him."

Lucilius moaned in agony, and Mark felt pity well up inside him. But he knew allowing Lucilius time to heal would be counterproductive, and he aimed at his heart and pulled the trigger.

He walked back to the car, where Isabella and Josephine stood waiting for him.

"You should have left," he told them. Isabella looked at him in confusion.

"That's not what you told us to do."

"But that's what you should have done."

"We should have left you behind?" Josephine asked with a frown.

"I don't know why, but you're very important. More important than me, so, yeah, you should have left me behind."

Mark could see that his statement didn't sit well with Josephine. He opened the driver's side of the car when he heard a siren, and a police car pulled up in front of them.

"Put the gun down, Mr. Reynolds. I knew you were a killer."

Theo leaped out of the van with his gun aimed at Mark.

"It's not what you think, Theo."

"Drop the gun. I won't say it again."

Mark slowly placed the MP7 on the hood of the car and put his hands up.

"Hands behind your back."

"We really need to get out of here, Theo."

"Hands behind your back."

Mark could see Theo was nervous, but he was more worried about the two bodies on the street. They could get up at any moment, and while he may have gotten the drop on them this time, he didn't see that happening again, at least not soon. Theo's gun wavered as he glanced over his shoulder at the two bodies on the ground.

"Officer," Isabella tried to bring out her I.D., and Theo aimed the gun at her.

"Stay back, ma'am." Theo turned back to Mark. "I'm placing you under arrest, Reynolds."

Mark kept his hands up, but he could see Lucilius's body twitching on the ground. Isabella saw it too, and her eyes opened wide in surprise.

"Oh, my God," she muttered.

Theo's gun wavered between Mark and Isabella, but he could see that Isabella was looking over his shoulder.

"Please, we need to go. Please," Isabella begged.

"If you value your life, Theo, get out of here now," Mark said.

He didn't want any harm to come to Theo. Not because he considered Theo a friend but because Gen cared for him. Mark could see the look of uncertainty in his eyes as he tried to keep the gun aimed at Mark.

Lucilius had stopped twitching, and he jerked upright on the ground. He groaned as he struggled to his feet, and the sound finally caused Theo to spin around.

He stared as Lucilius got to his feet. Remus heaved a sigh of relief as air entered his lungs, and he could breathe again. From the corner of his eye, Theo saw Mark pick up his assault weapon, but he didn't have the guts to stop him. It seemed he had stumbled into something beyond his understanding.

He remembered getting to Gen's ranch and seeing his father's broken body—he had felt a kind of fear then.

Mark stood calmly beside him and cradled his MP7 in his hands with the muzzle pointing downward.

"We will meet again, Protector," Lucilius said, then he and Remus turned and walked away.

"You need to leave here now, Theo," Mark said as he walked back to his car and opened the driver's door.

"You aren't going anywhere. You're under arrest." Theo was so angry that his voice shook. Mark got into his car and started it while Isabella and Josephine hurriedly got into the back seat.

"Get out of here," Mark warned. "They could be back."

Theo just watched as they drove off. He heard the wailing of sirens in the distance and decided staying wouldn't make any sense. Someone must have called the police, and this wasn't his jurisdiction anyway.

Theo got into his van and drove off.

They were completely surrounded.

Gen stopped counting after reaching twenty men. The exit was blocked, and men in black suits lined the walls like figurines on a mantelpiece, all holding weapons. She could see guns, clubs, and machetes. The men surrounding them looked fearsome, but

Gen didn't think their numbers were keeping the frown on her grandfather's face. The men didn't look like they could pull a rabbit out of a hat; this was the muscle. So, where was the big shot? Where was the one who brought sweat to her armpits and fear to her soul? It couldn't be any of these meatheads.

The men blocking the exit parted, and someone walked into the warehouse. The person appeared like a black spot in Gen's vision—not a shadow within a shadow or one surrounded with darkness. No, this was a huge black spot where the man should be.

He came out of the shadows and approached her and Myrddin. Gen struggled to switch off her spiritual awareness and saw that the man standing a couple of feet from Gen and her grandfather was short. Not average height; really short.

He looked misshapen and toadlike. He seemed to waddle as he approached, but Gen didn't need a seer to tell her that the man before her was the source of the blackness she had seen.

"Ah, the great Myrddin, or should I call you Merlin, as the world knows you?" His voice sounded whiny, as though he spoke through his nose.

"Asmodeus. I thought you were banished to the deepest part of Hades."

Gen frowned at her grandfather's words and leaned toward him. "Who is this?"

"This is one of the seven princes of hell, Asmodeus."

"Asmodeus? From hell? Then he's a…"

"Yes, a demon. And not just your average garden variety. This is one of the most powerful demons in Hades."

"And it knows your name?"

"We crossed paths once. Don't be fooled. This is but the skin he wears. He is hideous, but he is powerful."

Gen had to admit that Asmodeus didn't look frightening in any way.

"Why does he look…that way?"

"His essence cannot fit into our fleshy body, so he has to enter bodies to manifest on this plane. This is what his powers do. No matter the body he inhabits, the outcome is the same."

Gen noticed an object tucked into Asmodeus's belt; it had a dull shine as it reflected some of the ambient light. From its position tucked into the demon's belt, she guessed it was a knife. It took some seconds before she realized she was staring at one of the nails that was used to crucify Jesus Christ.

Asmodeus followed Gen's gaze to the nail on his belt and smiled.

"I have better use for this than that rabid dog. This was the bait to bring you here."

Gen still wasn't impressed with Asmodeus. So, he had all the whole bad boss motif going on, but he didn't look that scary.

What was she missing? What was there about this toadlike creature that made her grandfather's knees tremble in fear?

Even so, she flinched as his gaze penetrated her being.

"Ah, the nail bearer. I have been made aware of your rise to your office. Unfortunately for you, you won't survive this night."

"You're not the only one that has made such empty promises, and as you can see, I'm still standing," Gen spat.

Asmodeus chuckled.

"Did you just compare me to Lucilius and his band of miscreants? You do me a disservice, Genesis Isherwood. Would you compare a flea to an elephant or a worm to a leviathan? I am Asmodeus of the seventh realm of Hades. And you have reason to fear me."

Asmodeus grew before Gen's very eyes. His neck elongated, and his eyes became huge slits that pierced into her soul.

"Begone!" Gen screamed in defiance, and darkness consumed her.

Gen needed a fix.

The yearning was back, and her hand shook as she stared at herself in the bathroom mirror.

No!

This can't be real. She had gotten over molly.

Her head pounded.

How can this be?

Her stomach was cramped with pain.

She needed molly badly. She would do anything to feel the peace the drug brought.

Her eyes were their normal grey colour, though bloodshot. A memory teased at the corner of her mind, and she tried to grasp it, but the twisting of her stomach was too painful to ignore.

Had something happened to her eyes? Something made them change colour. She couldn't for the life of her remember what it was, but she knew it was important.

The clanging of different metals rang in Myrddin's ears along with the screaming of dying people around him.

He had caused this. By his power, the field around him was laid bare, scored by the eternal flames he had summoned to decimate the army that tried to conquer his land.

He was king, and the people should bow to power.

Someone groaned at his feet, and Myrddin looked down. He formed a spear of compressed air and plunged it into the chest of the soldier who was trying to crawl away from the bringer of death.

The soldier's blood splattered his face. He grinned.

They should fear him. Today, they would know what it would cost them in blood.

He would rain down destruction of a magnitude that would go down in history, and his name would be engraved in the annals of humanity.

He would show them no mercy.

Myrddin's smile turned fierce, but a face flashed before him for an instant—a toddler stumbling on a wooden floor as she tried to take her first steps.

He heard the sound of love and laughter and praise for the little girl. It filled him, and he clenched his head in pain.

What sorcery had the enemy channelled against him?

He was the mountain that the raging storm couldn't move.

The wind of destruction that laid waste to cities.

Why would the image of an unknown child bring such joy to his soul?

The men in suits circled Myrddin and Gen as they both groaned on their knees, lost in the hallucinations Asmodeus had spun them in. Tears trickled down Gen's cheeks as she relived a horror in her past. Myrddin covered his ears with his hands, his face twisted in silent rage as he wallowed in anguish.

They were lost in Asmodeus's world.

Mark didn't believe in coincidences.

He looked at his rear-view mirror as he headed back to the Triple 7 ranch. He wasn't being followed, but this knowledge didn't bring any peace to his mind.

The enemy knew the ranch. There was a bloody fight there not too long ago.

Could they have headed there also?

Were Gen and Myrddin safe?

Had this been a trap orchestrated by Lucilius and Remus?

He played back the fight in his mind and realized that Lucilius and Remus had seemed surprised to see him at Josephine's apartment.

Could it really have been a coincidence? But why had they targeted Josephine?

How had they known Josephine was important to Gen?

They could have killed her at any time in the past. Why wait until now?

Isabella and Josephine sat in the back of the car in silence. Mark looked in the rear-view mirror again, and his eyes locked with Josephine's. He could see the terror on her face.

Mark couldn't blame them. His present world wasn't a thing he would wish on anyone. He lived on the edge, but his responsibility as protector to Gen was something he was glad to have found.

He had come to realize that he had a strong sense of duty. Enlisting as a soldier now seemed like an inevitability, but he soon learnt that politics and bureaucracy were an ugly part of life. Systems that weighed human life against material gain were something he hadn't been able to stomach.

He found his sense of duty again when he met Gen. And stumbling on Lucilius and Remus meant the enemy was back, knocking on their door again, and he knew this fight was his purpose.

Isabella tried to still her shaking hand.

What had she stumbled into? She couldn't believe what she had seen. The past few hours were like a scene from a *Terminator* movie.

The dead literally rose to their feet.

And who was the man driving them to safety?

He could be trusted; that much was evident—they owed their lives to his intervention.

But why had he been there in Josephine's apartment? How did he know she was in trouble?

Had he and the two freaking zombies once worked together?

Isabella frowned.

That put a new twist on the whole situation. If it was only a falling out, how much could their saviour be trusted?

Gen knew she had to fight.

Something wasn't right. She had beaten molly. She knew she had. Random images flashed through her mind. She saw herself jogging on the streets of Dundurn. Striking an anvil!

Look at your wrists.

The whispered words drove her to look down, and she gasped. She held a razor blade in her right hand, and blood gushed from deep cuts in her wrists.

No! She screamed inaudibly as she dropped the blade and tried to stop the flow of the blood pouring from her body.

She wouldn't kill herself.

She had thought about it—when she was at her weakest—but she had been able to resist the urge.

Warm blood flowed down her hand. She felt light-headed.

She shook her head as she tried to remain conscious. *This wasn't real.*

Suddenly, a bright light filled her bathroom, and Gen had to squint to avoid the glare. She felt bathed in a warm glow, and the desire to end her life receded.

A being stepped into her vision and stretched out a hand to her. A finger touched her forehead, and the world burned bright in an instant.

Gen was on her knees, looking around the warehouse. The men in black suits staggered back from the light surrounding her. Myrddin was on his knees beside her, and she gripped his shoulder. For an instant, Gen saw regret in her grandfather's eyes. His shoulders were slumped in defeat; whatever memory he had just lived through weighed him down.

"It wasn't real. Whatever you saw was the enemy," she whispered.

Myrddin looked up at her in sorrow. "Not everything."

But he seemed to shake off the gloom, get to his feet, and help Gen up.

Asmodeus still stood some feet from them, but a twisted sneer filled his face.

"Why do you intervene?"

It was then that Gen noticed they weren't alone in the midst of the enemies around them. A being towered over them. It blazed with white light, so bright that Gen was surprised she could look at him. Her grandfather didn't seem worried about the being in light standing by their side, which gave her comfort in that.

Whatever this being was, if it was against the evil before her, she was okay with that.

"You will not always protect them, Baraqiel," Asmodeus spat in anger, then took a step back and disappeared. They were alone in the warehouse.

How powerful is Asmodeus? she wondered. *And where are the men in suits?*

The light beside her dimmed until a man's figure was clearly visible.

"It is good to see you, Myrddin," Baraqiel spoke in a rumbling voice.

Gen felt her spirit stagger and shake in resonance with his words. She noticed that she couldn't make out any of Baraqiel's features. She knew he was there, but she couldn't see his face.

"Thank you for your help, Baraqiel."

"You know him?" Gen asked gently.

Her grandfather still seemed shaken by what he had seen in his nightmare.

"I've met him once in my life, at a turning point in my existence. Baraqiel doesn't speak much. I'm sure you felt the impact of his words in your spirit. That's him at his lowest pitch."

"Is he…"

"Yes, he is."

"Why can't I see him? I know he's there, and I can make out his outline, but I can't see him."

"That's another thing with him. I don't think we have the capacity to withstand his essence. Either that, or he's trying to be mysterious."

Baraqiel chuckled, causing Gen to grimace as though she had sucked on a lime.

She saw her grandfather rub the back of his neck.

"What's wrong?"

"It's been a long time since I've been at the whipping end of the stick. And both times, Asmodeus had a hand in it."

"You've fought him before?" Gen asked.

"Not exactly. He drove a whole village to madness and rage, and I was forced to put a stop to it."

"A whole village?"

Myrddin didn't reply, and Gen let the matter drop. She could see that Myrddin was still not himself.

"Asmodeus is fear incarnate," Baraqiel said. "His strength comes from fear, and only with the words of the Creator resonating inside you can you stand against him. He dwells in your past mistakes, and while he may remind you of your past, it is wise to remember your future…and his."

Gen wiped her nose with the back of her hand. She expected to see blood on it from the pressure exerting on her body and soul due to Baraqiel's words and the timbre of his voice.

Thank God Baraqiel wasn't the one sent to deliver the good news to the Virgin Mary or her cousin, Elizabeth...or anyone for that matter.

Baraqiel turned in Gen's direction, and she felt the pressure increase.

"Greater is He that is in you."

She tried to nod, but her head was throbbing from the vibration coming from him.

"Why are you here, Baraqiel? Not that I'm ungrateful for your intervention," Myrddin said.

Baraqiel studied them for a moment. Gen could see he had dimmed his spiritual essence as much as possible; he now radiated a soothing feeling that steadied her nerves.

"A darkness is coming. Evil spreads its tentacles deep into your world." Baraqiel spoke in short sentences, pausing between each to allow them to recover from the force of his words.

"I was sent to let you know that you are not forgotten, nor are you alone. The princes of darkness are at work, and we are here to fight them. Stand strong and stand sure."

Suddenly, the pressure dissipated as quickly as it had come, and Gen found herself alone with her grandfather.

They had fallen into a trap, just as Mark had warned.

Thinking his name made her realize something else: If a trap had been set for her, was Mark safe?

6

CONSTANTINOPLE, 327 A.D.

Merlin hadn't been able to track down Hyginos. The man still moved from inn to inn, gathering crowds at market corners and spreading the same lies against the emperor. His seditious statements had begun to garner interest among disgruntled members of the senate, and the signs of an insurrection stirring were clear.

Queen Helena had told Merlin everything the prisoner and her son had said, and he immediately suspected the accursed's hand in the political turmoil within the city. He had left the palace as soon as he heard the news; the sooner Hyginos was stopped, the better.

So, Merlin sat in the corner of a tavern, sipping wine that tasted like sour milk, and waited for something to happen. Though he hadn't had any luck so far, a reliable source informed him that Hyginos frequented this tavern, and he hoped that would be the case this night.

The tavern was rowdy, the exact atmosphere to be expected from an establishment that catered to the lowlifes and the despicable. Men laughed, jeered, and drank.

Watered-down wine passed hands, arguments simmered, and fights were stopped by the tavern owner, a burly man with an imposing physique. Merlin tried not to scratch his beard as he watched. His keen eye tracked everyone who walked in alone and the groups that clustered together inside.

A simple spell meant every sound in the tavern was amplified and filtered in his direction. It made the boisterous noise even louder, but it was a small price to pay if it helped put a stop to the nefarious activities of the accursed. A man with a look of authority entered through the heavy wooden door and surveyed the tavern. Merlin noted that his clothes, though simple, looked new and clean—a sharp contrast to the attire of every other person inside. Merlin himself had made sure to collect a cloak that had seen better days to make sure he didn't stand out. The newcomer walked to the opposite corner of the tavern and joined two men who barely glanced at him at a table.

"You're late," one of them stated.

"I had to make sure I wasn't followed," the new guy informed them.

Merlin sipped his wine and tried to look disinterested.

"Did the shipment arrive?" the second man asked.

The newcomer looked around the tavern but didn't notice Merlin, who smiled at the barmaid, raising his wooden cup for a refill. "The shipment was offloaded at the designated spot we chose," he replied, lowering his voice.

"And it's enough to arm everyone?"

The newcomer bristled under the barrage of questions. "Do you doubt my competence? I assured you of enough weapons to arm a legion, and I have delivered. Now make sure you keep your end of the agreement," he snapped.

"That won't be a problem. If it's a rebellion the senate wants, a rebellion they shall get."

"Quiet!" the newcomer hissed. "Such words shouldn't come out of your lips. Not if you value your lives."

"Are you threatening us?" the first man snarled.

"I do not make threats, but I can assure you that when I do, I back them up. A wind of change is blowing, and it would be wise to remember that so that you don't get blown away."

With that, the newcomer stood up and left the tavern.

Merlin gritted his teeth in annoyance. He hoped the three men would all leave together; now, he had to decide which one to follow.

He dropped a silver coin on the table and left, spotting the newcomer walking down the street. He followed at a discreet distance. If he could identify this man, he could pass the information to Queen Helena and possibly the emperor.

The newcomer turned over his shoulder and slowed his pace. Merlin quickly cast a spell, and the area around him darkened. After a moment, the man resumed walking and almost immediately ducked into an alley.

Merlin frowned. The alley led to the seedier part of the city, and Merlin didn't think the newcomer resided there. Maybe he was on his way to meet another group?

As he turned into the alley, he felt the air ripple. A dagger sailed toward him.

Merlin flicked his hand, creating a gust of wind that diverted the dagger's path away from his heart. The newcomer hissed. He missed the target, and the thrust had unbalanced him, but he quickly recovered his balance and came at Merlin again. He held a new dagger with assurance, and the grin on his face revealed he expected an easy target.

While Merlin couldn't boast of being an expert in swordplay or unarmed combat, he was a proficient wizard and knew enough about warfare. He allowed the newcomer to make his move and created a lance of hardened air, deflecting the dagger thrust to the side. The newcomer's eyes opened wide when he saw the display of magical finesse. He decided to end the fight quickly and

rushed at Merlin, swinging recklessly in the hope of catching him unaware. Merlin dodged the swings and swept the newcomer's feet with his air-hardened lance. The man fell on his back, and Merlin moved in, aiming the lance at the man's throat.

"Who are you?" the man asked.

"The very question on my mind," Merlin replied.

"You are meddling with things beyond your understanding, Magician." The man struggled to his feet, and Merlin allowed him to get up.

"I'll ask again. Who are you, and why do you want to overthrow the emperor?"

The man frowned. He seemed annoyed Merlin knew about his conversation with the two men at the tavern. He opened his mouth to reply when Merlin heard a thud, and blood spewed out of the newcomer's mouth. The man stared down in surprise at the arrow protruding from his chest. Another thud, another arrow. He staggered from the force of the blows and fell to the ground as Merlin saw their attacker at the other end of the alley, now aiming at him.

Merlin turned away just in time, and the arrow sailed harmlessly down the alley. When he looked back, the alley was empty.

Merlin sighed.

He needed to get to Hyginos as quickly as possible.

Queen Helena took comfort in the fact that she knew she was dreaming. The past few days had been hectic as she tried to diffuse the harm Hyginos was doing with his words of treason and treachery. Her son was furious and had made Hyginos an enemy of the empire. Edicts were issued for his arrest, which Helena was sad to hear about.

Her numerous attempts to explain to Emperor Constantine fell on deaf ears, and she knew that the Christian community in the city was on the precipice of being declared a treasonous organization.

She had gone to bed with her heart weighed down by the burdens she had to carry. She kept the remaining foot nail under her pillow and clenched it tight; it was a source of comfort and protection against the forces of darkness.

As she slept, Helena felt a cool breeze across her cheeks. She was in the midst of a crowd gathered by a lake, who all sat in rapt attention listening to the man on a boat by the seashore.

Helena listened to Jesus's teachings with the rest of the people around her.

"The kingdom of God can be likened to a man who sowed good seeds in his field. While the man slept, an enemy came and sowed tares among the seeds. When the good seeds grew, behold, the tares grew with the seeds. Then the servants came to the master and informed him of the development. Sir, they said, did you not grow good seeds in your field? From where did these tares come?"

Jesus paused and looked at the faces of the people gathered listening to Him.

"The master answered the servants and told them that an enemy had done this. The servants wanted to go and weed out the tares, but the master stopped them, saying that they would most likely weed out the blades of the good seeds as well. The master told the servants to allow the good seeds and the tares to grow together until the time of harvest. That during the harvest, the tares would be gathered together in bundles and burnt, but the wheat should be put into the master's barn."

Helena allowed Jesus's words to sink into her soul. The parable seemed to resonate with her present predicament, and she was sure this vision was a message.

She needed to look inward for the source of the problem. If she understood correctly, the enemy was in their midst.

Calisto didn't like leaving Queen Helena's side, but the information he had received made it imperative. Ever since the emperor's edict, Hyginos's family had disappeared into thin air, and Calisto had been secretly searching for them. He had sent word to his network of spies and soldiers, and a reply had come back— Hyginos's elder sister had been found.

He had hoped she would lead him to Hyginos, and ordered his men to track her, but either she had spotted them, which Calisto didn't think was possible, or she didn't know where her younger brother was.

It was night when he left, and most of the citizens were asleep. The few who weren't steered clear and allowed him to hurry down the street. The night air cooled the thin film of sweat on his arms as he went.

He stopped at a small house. A guard emerged from the shadows across the street and gently thumped his fist to his chest in acknowledgement of his presence.

"Is she still in there?" Calisto asked.

"She is."

"And she is alone?"

"Yes. A man came earlier, but he didn't stay long. Cato shadowed him, but he was only an associate."

He gripped the guard's shoulder to show his appreciation and knocked loudly on the door. He waited, then knocked again and heard shuffling from inside. He hoped the woman wouldn't make a run for it; that would only spell her guilt and possibly her doom at the hands of interrogators.

The door opened, and a woman stared at Calisto with sleepy eyes.

"Marcella?"

She tried to shut the door against him, but Calisto shoved it, and the woman stumbled. He entered a tiny room with just a single bedroll in a corner.

"Where is Hyginos?" Calisto could see fear written all over the woman's face.

She wore a blue dress and a scarf over her head. He couldn't be sure of her age, she looked middle-aged, but the fine lines around her eyes could be due to stress or labour rather than age.

"I do not know."

"That's hard to believe since your whole family has gone to great lengths to disappear. Where is he?"

"I do not know where Hyginos is. I swear by the great gods. I haven't heard from him in a while."

"And when last did you speak to Hyginos?"

"About a week ago?"

"And how was he?"

The woman frowned, clearly confused by the question. She reflexively tucked a stray strand of hair into the scarf.

"I do not understand your question, great sir."

"What was his disposition like? Was he angry? Confused? Scared? Did he seem different from his normal self?"

"I do not see how…" The woman paused as doubt flashed across her face. "He seemed very sure of himself. Very unafraid. I assumed he must have wealthy and influential backers, so I didn't think much of it."

"Why would such behaviour stand out?"

"You must understand, Hyginos is very timid. He stammers when he is emotional. That day, he spoke like a king. He seemed too self-assured, and I remember asking him if he had suddenly become rich."

Calisto rubbed his chin. He was certain the man she had seen wasn't her younger brother.

One of the accursed could change his appearance like a chameleon changes its colour. Hyginos was either captured and imprisoned somewhere or, more likely, he was dead.

Calisto left the house hurriedly. He needed to get back to the palace immediately and discuss the situation. Maybe Merlin could provide a solution, a way to counter the accursed before they threw the whole city into chaos?

7

Martha Isherwood was waiting on the porch when Mark drove into the ranch. She walked toward him as he switched off the engine and got out, with Josephine and Isabella following.

"Is she back?" he asked.

Martha shook her head and turned questioningly to Josephine and Isabella.

"This is Josephine Baddock and Isabella—" Mark started.

"Isabella from the *Daily Sun.*" Isabella shook hands with Martha while Josephine waved shyly from behind her.

Mark looked at the road and tried to stem the tendrils of worry rising in his heart.

She's okay. Myrddin is with her. She's protected.

He followed Mrs. Isherwood, who was leading the two women into the house, but spun back when he heard the sound of a car approaching. He couldn't stop his sigh of relief, but his smile slipped when he saw the worried look on Myrddin's face.

Gen got out of the car and hugged Mark. Over Gen's head, he looked questioningly at Myrddin, who shook his head, indicating that they would talk later.

"I was so worried," Gen said.

"So was I."

They held each other for a little longer and then reluctantly pulled apart.

"You were right!" they both said at the same time, and Mark smiled ruefully.

"You first," Gen urged.

"You were right. Miss Baddock was in danger. I bumped into our old pals, Lucilius and Remus."

"No." She looked Mark over.

"I'm okay. I didn't stay long for a chat. An hour later and Josephine Baddock would have been dead. Seems Lucilius and Remus are working for somebody. That gives me the jitters just thinking about it."

"I think we met their boss," Gen said.

"You met...come again?"

"It was a trap, Mark, and we walked into it. Almost didn't make it out."

"You are good?"

"Yeah. Let's talk inside." Gen held Mark's hand as they walked into the house.

Josephine and Isabella were already in the living room; each sat with a mug of coffee in their hands.

They looked up when Gen and Mark entered the room, and Gen could see her staring at their clasped hands. She tried not to read any meaning in that look. She wasn't going to hide her feelings for Mark anymore and, with all that had happened to them, every day was a blessing that shouldn't be wasted.

"This is Josephine Baddock," Mark introduced the woman they had risked their lives—Mark's life—to save.

Josephine's spiritual essence shimmered brightly in Gen's inner sight. She was definitely the same woman she had seen in her vision, one of the seven. Now, all Gen needed to do was figure out why she was so important that the enemy wanted her dead. The woman beside Josephine stood up and stretched out her hand as she introduced herself.

"Hi, I'm Isabella from the *Daily Sun*."

Isabella's essence formed a dull grey mist seeping out of her mouth.

Hmm, that's new, Gen thought. She felt that Isabella's smile seemed false, and it hit her.

"That's not true."

Isabella looked at Gen warily and saw that she had the attention of everybody in the room. The old man with laugh lines around his eyes frowned.

"Excuse me?" Isabella said warily.

"You were lying just now. You aren't from the *Daily Sun*. Who are you?"

She noticed Mark tense as he had at Josephine's apartment.

"Wait a minute. I can explain. I really am a reporter." Isabella was confused. How did Gen know? And who was Gen anyway? She wore dark sunglasses even though she was indoors, and her face looked vaguely familiar.

"Explain yourself, young girl," said the older man. She couldn't remember the last time she was called a young girl, and if the situation hadn't seemed so fatal, she would have laughed.

"I'm a reporter for the *Quest*. We are a small…"

"Again, you're lying," Gen said. "I must assume you've met Mark. He can be…somewhat overprotective and, let me tell you a truth: he takes his job very seriously."

Isabella felt her throat go dry, and she immediately recognized the feeling of fear that gripped her heart as she stared into Mark's eyes.

"Okay. I really am a reporter. I run a blog, and a podcast too. I was hoping there was a story regarding the incident at St. Philip's Memorial Hospital that could boost my career."

She stared down at her feet as she spoke.

"A blog?" Gen asked.

"And a podcast. That's the truth."

"I know," Gen said.

While she wasn't sure that having a reporter in

their midst was safe, Gen knew this was the truth, and she felt in her gut that Isabella would play an important role.

She shook her head slightly when Mark glanced at her, and he relaxed his guard, but she could still feel his anger boiling like the sun on a hot summer day. She squeezed his arm to let him know she understood how he felt and turned to Josephine.

"Welcome to the Triple 7 ranch. I don't know how to phrase this, so I'll say it straight and hope you understand." Gen could see she had Josephine's attention. Unfortunately, Isabella seemed to be hanging on her every word, too, but that couldn't be helped.

"Two weeks ago, I was at St. Philip's, hoping to stop Mark from dying." She wasn't sure how much information she could give Josephine but felt she should go with her gut feeling. "Mark was dying. Already dead, actually, from a sword stabbed into his heart."

Josephine and Isabella looked skeptical. Isabella's doubt, Gen could understand, but Josephine had been healed of terminal cancer. She expected her to relate to the supernatural better than Isabella.

"I know it's hard to believe, but that's the truth. Mark's right here as a witness to the fact. I had a vision while I was in hospital, and I saw you." Gen tried to smile to ease Josephine's fears. She knew it was hard to take in, but she didn't have time to hold anyone's hand. She had seen what Asmodeus could do, and they needed to be ready.

"In my vision, Josephine, you helped me fight a great darkness that is coming. A darkness brought about by an evil group, and I heard you've met two of them."

Josephine nodded slowly.

"You met two immortals when they came to your apartment. Yes, immortals. They've been around for millennia, and they've hounded generations for hundreds of years. They don't die easily, a fact I'm sure you can testify to."

Josephine raised her hand.

"You're free to ask any question," Gen smiled.

"Why me?"

"I don't know. I've asked myself that very question, but I've come to understand something. The question you should be asking yourself is, why not you?"

Gen had come to realize and accept that she had been trusted with something great: a chance to change the world.

Josephine gave a deep nod, and Gen could tell she was willing to accept the truth. She turned to see Isabella fidgeting in her seat and sighed.

"Yes, Isabella?"

"If you had said all this two hours ago, I would have called you crazy, and I'm still not convinced that isn't a viable theory."

"And your question is?"

"How come no one else knows about all this? You're saying a great darkness was coming, and you have to fight against it with Josephine's help. That seems a little farfetched."

"If you stick around long enough, you'll get to find out how real it is."

Myrddin walked up to Gen and Mark and leaned close. "I think we need to sit down and talk," he whispered.

"We'll talk more soon. Please, make yourselves at home," Gen offered. "Unfortunately, we have only one guest room, so if both of you don't mind sharing, you're welcome to it."

"We'll be staying here?" Josephine asked.

"Are we prisoners?" Isabella added.

"It will be safer for you if you remain here for the time being. You can leave any time you want, but I wouldn't advise it. I'll be back in a moment."

Gen felt exhausted. She couldn't believe taking care of others could be this fatiguing. She walked to the kitchen with Mark and her grandfather and immediately flopped into a chair.

"That was tiring," Gen moaned.

"You did great," Mark said as he sat down opposite her. "Sounded like my sergeant just before we went on a mission. Straight and precise."

Gen smiled at Mark's attempt at levity and watched her grandfather sit beside Mark.

"What really happened, Mark?" Myrddin asked.

Mark quickly filled them in on what transpired at Josephine's house.

"Theo was there?" Gen asked.

"Yeah. I think we may need to bring him in before he does something stupid or gets caught in the crossfire," Mark said.

Gen nodded and told her side of the story.

"You met a…demon?"

"Not just a demon, Mark, one of the seven princes of hell," Myrddin said. "Asmodeus is a fallen angel. His power comes from fear. He can make you relive your worst nightmare. He sows seeds of doubt and discrimination. He is a moving plague and a harbinger of death and destruction."

"Sounds like a real piece of work. So, how do we deal with him?"

Mark believed everyone had a weakness that could be exploited. If they had survived immortal beings bent on killing them, they could survive a prince of hell.

"I don't know if he has a weakness, Mark," Myrddin announced as though he had read Mark's mind. "I have encountered him once, and only the intervention of Baraqiel made it possible to banish him."

"The same angel that came to your aid today? I think we're not as helpless as we believe. And what did Baraqiel say again?" Mark said.

"Only with the words of the Creator resonating in you can you be victorious, well, he actually said stand against him, but I'm figuring that means winning," Gen said.

"So, we stand against the bastard when he comes. We face up to our deepest and darkest fears so that he doesn't have anything to use against us," Mark said.

Gen felt her despair vanish in the face of Mark's optimism. She knew Mark would never give up. He would never back down when it came to protecting her. She had to do the same for him.

"Asmodeus is still formidable without his power of fear. He can't be hurt by any weapon known to man," Myrddin said.

"But we also have a weapon that can harm any evil. We have the foot nail," Mark stated.

The nails were transformed by the blood of Jesus Christ and were powerful enough to destroy any evil. Out of the three used to crucify him, the foot nail was the most powerful.

It was back in the anvil in the barn, protected by Myrddin's concealment spell.

"We need to bring in the doctor immediately," Myrddin suggested.

Gen and Mark nodded in agreement.

"I think I'll be the one to do that. And, before either of you think of arguing, this will be the one time I won't be reasoned with," Myrddin said with a note of finality.

There was a moment of silence as the three pondered their next move.

"I think it'll be safe to say that we'll be expecting some visitors soon," Mark said.

"Then it will be unbecoming of us if we don't give them a befitting welcome," Myrddin said with a wicked smile.

✦

Myrddin walked to the reception desk in St. Philip's Memorial Hospital and smiled at the tall woman with dreadlocks standing behind it.

"Hello, my name is Myrddin. I would like to see Doctor David O'Neal."

After a pause, the receptionist returned his smile; she must have decided he was harmless.

"Do you have an appointment?" Gina asked.

"We were referred, no, my granddaughter was referred to him by Doctor Burham. Regarding her eyes."

Gina clicked open her computer and tapped some keys.

"There's no appointment here. You'll need to wait to see him."

"I can do that."

The receptionist still had a smile on her face as she watched Myrddin walk to the chairs by the wall and join the group of people waiting to see their doctors.

Mark walked to Myrddin's mini-workshop in the barn. He pulled up a suitcase from under the work-table, placed it on the surface, and unzipped it. He retrieved an MP7, his Glock .45, two flash grenades, and a combat knife with a steel tip and placed them all on the table.

Finally, he brought out a sword and sheath. Myrddin had crafted the sheath for him, one he could strap behind his back. He swirled it around, getting used to its weight as it swished through the air. It was a special sword; he had won it from the immortal Lucilius during their last fight.

Myrddin's mind kept drifting to his encounter with Asmodeus as he waited for Doctor O'Neal. He needed to face his fears, the evil he had wrought. He was a different man then, but that didn't change the facts.

People died.

He could still smell the charred bodies and the metallic tang of blood that had soaked the earth around him.

That was his past. He had to move on if he was going to be of any use in the coming battle.

Myrddin looked up as a handsome man in his early thirties dressed in doctor's scrubs walked up to him.

"I'm Doctor O'Neal. What seems to be the problem?"

"Good to see you. My name is Myrddin, and what I have to say to you can only be said in private."

"Gina said you were referred to me by Doctor Burham."

Myrddin nodded.

"Follow me."

He followed the doctor to his office and sat across from him.

"I only have a few minutes as I have to make my rounds. I don't know why Doctor Burham referred you to me, but since I owe him a favour, I'll hear you out. What's the problem?"

"This may sound strange, but I believe your life is in danger, and I need you to follow me."

Doctor O'Neal looked at Myrddin as though he'd escaped a psychiatric institution.

"I really do not have time for this. I have a patient who needs me to—"

Myrddin snapped his fingers, and a ball of fire rested a couple of inches above his palm. Doctor O'Neal's eyes grew round in amazement. He shook his head and stood up, then walked slowly toward Myrddin, never taking his eyes off the flame. He stretched out his hand to the fire and jerked back when he felt its heat.

"Impossible. How are you doing it?"

"I do not have the time to try to convince you, so I'm giving it to you straight. You are a man of science, and I can prove that what I'm about to tell you is real. You are in danger from people like me, and unless you follow me, you may not survive the day."

Myrddin snuffed out the flame.

"Wait, what do you mean?"

Myrddin cocked his head. He could hear Gina arguing with someone outside.

"Quick, we have to get out of here. They are here already."

The door burst open, and Lucilius and Remus stormed into the office. Remus pulled out his magical bow, and an arrow flew at Doctor O'Neal's chest. Myrddin swirled his hand, and a gust of wind deflected the arrow away from the doctor.

He clapped his hands together, and a storm slammed Lucilius and Remus against the wall.

"Give me your hand," Myrddin shouted at the doctor. Lucilius was struggling against the force of the wind but was dragging himself off the wall and toward Myrddin.

"Give me your hand if you want to live!"

He grabbed onto Doctor O'Neal, and in a flash, they disappeared.

Myrddin popped into existence in the hospital's parking lot. Doctor O'Neal released his held breath and staggered away from him.

"Get away from me. What are you? This is impossible." The doctor was on the verge of hysteria. Myrddin grabbed him by both arms and pulled him toward the car despite his thrashing protests.

"Listen to me, good doctor. I teleported us a few feet away, so we are not out of danger just yet. I need you to get your act together and get into the car immediately."

He opened the back door and shoved the struggling doctor through it, then dropped into the driver's seat and drove off just as Lucilius and Remus were running into the parking lot.

Gen heard the sound of an approaching car and rushed out of the house. At the same time, Mark emerged from the barn holding a pistol. The sheriff's van appeared in the drive, and Theo got out.

"Hey, Theo, what's up?" Gen tried to smile, but she couldn't get her face to respond.

"What's going on, Gen? And don't try and brush me off. I know something is going on, and you know more about my dad than you're telling."

"Theo, now isn't a good time."

"I'm not leaving here without an explanation." His hand moved to the holster on his hip when Mark walked toward him. "Stop there! You're under arrest."

Mark stopped beside Gen, who was glad to see he'd hidden his own gun away, likely beneath his shirt at his back.

"On what charges, Theo?"

"That's Deputy Cuttaham to you. I saw you run away from a crime scene."

"I could tell you it was all a hoax, and I was using a BB gun. There are no bodies, so you really don't have any grounds for your arrest."

Theo chewed his lower lip and turned to Gen. "What's going on? What have you gotten yourself into, Gen?"

"Something I don't want you involved in, Theo. There are bad people involved, and they wouldn't think twice about hurting you. I need you to leave. For your own good."

They heard footsteps on the porch, and they all turned to see Josephine and Isabella come out of the house.

"Who are these women, Gen? Are you running a cell?"

"Really, Theo?"

"You've changed, Gen. Ever since you came back to Dundurn from that university. Ever since you started moving with *him*," Theo nodded in Mark's direction. He walked toward Josephine and Isabella, his hand still on the tip of his gun. "Ladies, I need to ask you some questions, and you both need to follow me to the station."

Josephine looked from Theo to Mark.

"Look, Officer...Theo, is it? I don't know what you think is going on, but we are here of our own volition, and unless you have an arrest warrant or such, we will remain here where it's safe. I'd also advise you to listen to these two. They seem to know what they're doing."

Theo's expression of confusion grew as he looked from the two women to Gen and Mark. He opened his mouth to speak but was interrupted as Myrddin drove into the ranch.

Everyone stood still as he got out of the car and opened the door for Doctor O'Neal. The doctor looked around in confusion, still dazed.

"Granddad?"

Myrddin walked up to the group and noticed Theo with his hand still on his gun. "Young Theo Cuttaham. What are you doing here?"

"Mr. Gourdeau? You're…alive?"

"Obviously, Theo," Myrddin stated.

"But we attended your funeral."

"My memorial, young man. Heard it was nice."

"What's going on here?"

Mr. Gourdeau had died, but Theo realized he'd never seen the body. The memorial service was held without a coffin—because Mr. Gourdeau had been cremated, he thought.

"We have a slight predicament," Myrddin said. "We met Lucilius and Remus at the hospital. Luckily, I got there first and was able to extract the good doctor."

"What's wrong with him?" Mark asked, seeing the glazed look in the doctor's eyes.

"Had to teleport him to safety. I think he's having a life-defining moment."

"Did you just say teleport?" Theo asked in amazement.

"Yes. You have two choices, young Theophilus Cuttaham. You can remain here and have the answers you seek or go home and forget you ever heard this conversation. Which will it be?"

Theo gaped at them, and then a determined look crossed his face. "Are these people you are talking about involved in the attack on my dad?"

"Yes, they are, but that shouldn't …" Myrddin started.

"I'm in."

Myrddin took a moment to stare into Theo's eyes, and he must have been satisfied with what he saw because he nodded quickly and turned to Mark and Gen. "We have to prepare. Asmodeus will be coming here next."

Silence settled over the group. Gen and Mark nodded. Theo looked at the stern faces around him and raised his hand. "Who is Asmodeus?"

"Your worst nightmare," Mark informed him, patting Theo's shoulder as he and Gen walked away.

8

"We need to come up with a plan," Mark said. He, Myrddin, and Gen were in the kitchen, sipping coffee, ignoring Theo, who stood by the wall. He was doing his best to understand what was going on without looking insignificant. Myrddin grunted in affirmation while Gen nodded.

"I'll set up a containment spell around the house so that we don't attract any attention," Myrddin voiced.

"What can we expect this time?" Mark asked.

"I really don't know. Asmodeus is an unknown variant. The question we need to ask is, what do they want?"

"Apart from wanting us dead, I'd say they want the nail," Gen said. It seemed pretty straightforward to her.

"Let's not forget Josephine and Doctor O'Neal. They want them dead, too," Mark added.

Theo looked from one speaker to the other, his mind rebelling at what he was hearing.

"So, what do we do?" Gen asked.

"We hunker down and weather the storm, making it costly for them," Mark suggested.

"But can we survive Asmodeus? He is extremely powerful," Myrddin said.

"We have an angel on our side. That should even things out. The rest we can handle," Mark countered.

"It doesn't work that way. Baraqiel may intervene, or there may be a bigger picture we're not aware of."

"What could be greater than this? This has the whole end-of-the-world motif. We need his help," Mark stated.

Gen listened intently, but she couldn't shake the feeling they were missing something.

"Why would Lucilius and Remus go out of their way to try and kill Josephine and Doctor O'Neal?" she asked.

"Because they were ordered to," Mark said.

"Yes, but why? Why target the exact same people that I had the vision about?" Gen wondered aloud.

"We already established that they were important to you."

"Not to me, Mark. They're important to the fight, and the enemy knows that. That means the people I saw are more powerful than we realize. That's what the enemy saw, and that's why they were after them."

Silence settled over the kitchen as realization dawned on everyone there—everyone except Theo, who just followed the conversation, trying not to look ignorant or too shocked.

"I want to try something while we set up our defences," Gen said excitedly.

She rushed out of the kitchen with Mark and Myrddin on her heels and entered the sitting room to see Josephine sitting in a corner and Doctor O'Neal texting a message on his phone.

"I need the foot nail," Gen said, unsurprised when Mark pulled it out of his pocket. She had sensed the nail's presence on him ever since he left the barn.

Gen walked up to Josephine and sat beside her. "I can only imagine what you are going through right now," she said softly. "I was once lost and confused until I found a greater purpose. I think you're destined for greater things, too. My journey started with this object."

Mark sat beside Gen, holding the foot nail. Josephine stared at it.

"What is it?"

"It's one of the three nails used to crucify Jesus Christ."

Gen heard a sputter of laughter and turned to the doctor sitting across from them.

"Do you really still doubt, Doctor O'Neal? Even after all that happened today?" Myrddin asked.

Doctor O'Neal got to his feet and walked over.

"I'm to believe that what you have in your grasp is a nail from over two thousand years ago?"

"Haven't archaeologists dug up artifacts even older than this nail?" Myrddin countered. "What makes their evidence more believable than what you've seen or heard today?"

"Magic isn't real," O'Neal spat.

"But is today's science not yesterday's magic?"

"That's arguable. There must be a logical explanation for what you did at the hospital."

"There is. It's called belief. Belief in how God sees us."

O'Neal snorted but didn't argue the point. Gen sensed the nail's tug, but she no longer felt pulled helplessly toward it. Its purpose was to point to Christ, and she now had a deeper relationship with Him. It had served its goal for her, and she hoped it would do the same for Josephine and Doctor O'Neal.

Gen reached out and held Josephine's hand. With her other hand, she grabbed the nail from Mark.

The transition was smooth. Gen looked around and was relieved to see Josephine standing beside her. She hadn't been sure it would work, but she had hoped, and she was glad it had.

That meant her theory was correct.

"Where are we?" Josephine said, scared.

"It's okay. We're reliving a time in the life of Jesus Christ."

Gen heard voices and took the time to study her environment. They were in a house with a roof slanted so low that she could reach out and touch it if she stretched.

She and Josephine walked toward the voices and rounded a corner to see a table occupying a large part of the room. The people sitting around it were eating what looked like unleavened bread.

"I know this place. This is the Last Supper," Josephine whispered in awe.

She was right. Gen quickly spotted Jesus at the head of the table, and His disciples sat around Him to either side.

"I am the true vine, and my Father is the Husbandman. Every branch that doesn't bear fruit He takes away, but every branch that bears fruit, He prunes so that the branch can bear more fruit."

The words sunk deep into Gen's heart. She could feel the rapt attention of the disciples as they listened to Jesus's every word.

"You are clean because of the word which I have spoken to you. Abide in me, and I in you. As a branch cannot bear fruit by itself except if it remains on the vine, so, too, you cannot bear fruit except if you remain in me."

Gen felt the world swirl around them again.

"What's happening?" Josephine screamed. She reached out, and Gen held onto her hand.

"It's okay. Sometimes, it's more than one vision. We're safe."

The world settled again, and Gen looked around. They were by a small hillside, among a huge crowd. Gen and Josephine looked up to see Jesus sitting on the small hill.

"Blessed are the poor in spirit, for theirs is the kingdom of heaven. Blessed are they that mourn, for they shall be comforted. Blessed are the meek, for they shall inherit the earth. Blessed are they who hunger and thirst after righteousness, for they shall be filled. Blessed are the merciful, for they shall obtain mercy."

Jesus continued, but Gen felt the pull of reality beginning to exert itself on them. "We're returning," she told Josephine.

The sitting room steadied before them. Josephine flopped back on the sofa, and Gen gulped in air through her mouth as she tried to regain her senses.

"Was all that real?" Josephine uttered.

"Was what real? You just stood there holding hands," O'Neal barked.

"It's the power of the nail. It grants visions to the bearer of the nail. This is the first time I've seen someone else get carried along." Myrddin looked at Gen in amazement. His granddaughter was full of surprises. "How did you know you could do that?" he asked.

"It was a hunch. I kept wondering why Josephine and the doctor are important to Lucilius and his boss," she said.

"If they respond to the nail, maybe they have other hidden abilities, too," Mark added.

It made sense now.

With only Gen, they were able to disrupt the enemy's plan. How much more powerful would their group be if they had more people like Gen?

"All this is moot if we don't survive Asmodeus," Myrddin noted. He was glad they could add more people with abilities, but having abilities was one thing—knowing what to do with them was another.

Unless they were gifted like Gen, but then, Gen was the nail bearer. The last of a generation of nail bearers. Somehow, Myrddin didn't think anybody could hold up to her.

He knew what Asmodeus could do, and he prayed they were ready for him.

Myrddin stood in the middle of the Triple 7 ranch with his hands raised and sweat pouring from his body. He had completed the containment spell—the strongest spell he had ever had to conjure—and he hoped it would be enough to keep Asmodeus out of the ranch.

Myrddin modified the spell from the last time he cast one. While most containment spells allowed objects and entities in and kept them in, this one kept them out. And his spell covered the whole ranch.

It had been quite some time since he had taxed his body this much, and Myrddin needed to rest to recover his spent essence. He walked to the house and saw Mark come out of the barn with his sword strapped on his back.

Myrddin remembered simpler days when he was a ranch owner. He bred horses—not because he needed the money, but because he liked horses, and he needed a good alias.

He built the ranch one plank at a time, without using magic, relishing the feel of sawing and hammering the wood together.

"We have a wide area to cover," Mark stated when he reached Myrddin.

"Chances are that Asmodeus isn't the subtle type. He's going to come in hard and hope to subdue us all at once. Lucilius and Remus, on the other hand…"

"Are crafty bastards. We'll have to watch out for those two."

"That would be wise. I'll handle Asmodeus."

They reached the house, and Mark noted the spell surrounding the door. The whole ranch lit up in his new sight as he saw various sigils and marks at different points areas. "Will this hold?" he asked.

"It's a banishing spell. Any inhuman entity that crosses the door will be instantly banished from this world."

Mark accepted the statement, and they walked into the house. While the sitting room had two entry points, he felt it was safer to have every non-combatant in the same place, and the windows were all magically reinforced to make them unbreakable. They had convinced Gen's parents to book a room in an undisclosed motel in Saskatoon. Theo refused to leave, offering to stay and fight, and while his gesture was admirable, Mark felt he would be more of a liability than an asset—just one more person he'd have to keep an eye out for.

The only person who seemed to be buzzed by the impending attack was Isabella. She had taken to following Gen around wherever she went. Mark admonished her to remain in the sitting room should any fight break out.

Gen stood in the middle of the sitting room wearing black jeans and a matching top. She had removed her sunglasses, and Mark could see the stares from those who hadn't yet seen her newly-coloured eyes.

Mark walked up to her, "We're as ready as we can be," he smiled.

"Let's pray that's enough," Gen said. She smiled as her granddad patted her on the shoulder and slumped on the sofa, shutting his eyes and entering a meditative state.

Myrddin woke with a start. One of his barriers was destroyed. He had placed traps at both ends of the road leading to the ranch—tiny segments from his essence that triggered an alarm when crossed or destroyed. He stood up quickly. He wasn't fully rested, but that couldn't be helped. The enemy was on their doorstep.

"They are here," Myrddin stated.

No one asked if he was sure. Gen and Mark had an inclination toward his capabilities and didn't question his opinions.

"Do we know how many?" Mark asked. He flexed his shoulders and pulled his Glock .45 out of his side holster.

"I can't tell yet. They crossed one of the alarms I placed at the end of the road. They should be here any minute, though."

Myrddin could sense Asmodeus, even from this distance. There were two other presences with Asmodeus.

"Lucilius and Remus are with him, I think," he said.

Myrddin sensed they had stopped at the ranch's gate. "Seems they want to parley," he grunted.

He had expected Asmodeus to come in charging without regard for matters like terms of engagement or the offer to surrender.

"Let's hear what the man has to say then," Mark said.

"How many others are there, Granddad?"

Myrddin frowned. Unless the men with Asmodeus were so heavily cloaked that he couldn't sense them, it seemed like there were only three of them.

"I can't sense anyone else."

"He's here with only Lucilius and Remus?" Gen was surprised.

"Looks that way," Myrddin answered.

"Is he really that strong?" Mark asked.

Mark needed to assess the enemy, and the offer of peace talks was the best ground to do that. Was it a good tactic that Asmodeus came with only Lucilius and Remus? A show intended to intimidate them and make them lose morale?

"Let's go see what this prince of hell wants," he stated again.

Gen nodded, and they headed for the front door, leaving Theo and the others behind.

Asmodeus's short, toadlike figure stood in the middle of his men, with Lucilius and Remus flanking either side. Myrddin was surprised to see men in black suits waiting outside his containment area.

There was no way he could have missed the spiritual signature of more than twenty men. Was Asmodeus able to cloak that many people in invisibility?

He, Gen, and Mark stopped at the centre of the ranch and waited.

Mark studied the man standing between Lucilius and Remus, unimpressed. Myrddin and Gen had told him not to be fooled by Asmodeus's seemingly unassuming appearance, so he took an extra moment to study the man with his new gift.

Asmodeus reeked of magic. Dark, tainted, evil magic.

He saw what looked like tiny strings attached to the twenty men standing with Asmodeus.

Were they possessed? Was Asmodeus controlling them against their will?

"Asmodeus seems to be controlling these men like puppets," Mark said.

Myrddin frowned and scanned the men standing with Asmodeus. They all emitted the same evil, spine-chilling frequency as him.

Could they really be under Asmodeus's spell? But if they were, Myrddin should have detected their essence.

Then it hit Myrddin.

"The men are all simulacra," Myrddin said in amazement.

"What are you talking about?" Gen asked.

"What's a simu…whatever you said?" Mark said.

"A simulacrum. Every one of those men is just Asmodeus's essence. A better word would be clones or replicas but without individual souls. That's why I couldn't sense them. They are all Asmodeus."

Myrddin marvelled at Asmodeus's powers.

"They're all Asmodeus? So, what you're saying is that these men aren't really men?" Mark asked.

Myrddin nodded.

"Great. Then I don't have to be bothered about killing many versions of this asshole," Mark grinned.

"Let's not get ahead of ourselves. We are here for a parley. Let him talk."

Now that Myrddin knew what to look out for, he wouldn't fall the trick a second time. He, Mark, and Gen walked a little farther but stopped meters before the gate of the ranch.

"I was beginning to think the mighty Merlin, slayer of dragons and leviathans, was too scared to meet," Asmodeus taunted.

"What do you have to say, Asmodeus?" Myrddin asked.

"Give me the woman and the doctor and I will leave this miserable place and not end your short existence."

"You don't want the nail?" Gen had to know. How important were Josephine and Doctor O'Neal?

"You can keep your trinkets. After all, I have one with me." Asmodeus lifted a rope from around his neck—the second nail was tied to its end.

"I can also sense the other nail on the Protector, but as I said, you can keep your precious object. I have no need for it. Bring me the woman and the doctor, and we can all go our merry ways."

"You know we can't do that, Asmodeus. You can't be allowed to have free will here on earth," Myrddin said.

"And who will stop me?" Asmodeus laughed. "I have weighed you, magician, and I must confess, I am not impressed with what I see. You are just like every other mortal I have conquered. Weak and pathetic."

"I will stop you," Gen challenged. She looked at Asmodeus and didn't back down from his glare.

"You are broken, Nail Bearer. A little pressure, and I will shatter that fragile mind of yours."

"You can try Asmodeus, but you will find out that my will is stronger than before." Gen looked at Lucilius and Remus—two swirling masses of blackness to her new eyes.

Suddenly, she remembered one of her visions.

He who the Son sets free is free indeed.

While the words had made sense to her, they hadn't really connected until that moment.

She could set them free.

"You can be free," Gen whispered, but she might as well have shouted. Lucilius and Remus turned to her.

"You can be free," Gen said in a firmer voice.

It was the truth.

That's what she hadn't understood before. No one was too far gone that Jesus couldn't save.

Even the immortals.

"He can set you free. Lucilius, you can be free from the curse."

Myrddin and Mark turned to her in shock.

"Impossible! You lie, wench," Lucilius snarled. He lunged forward, but Asmodeus restrained him with a flick of his hand.

"Is that your gamble, Nail Bearer? Wishful delusions of grandeur? A hope to assuage the base emotions of humanity? They don't have it anymore. They are cut off to wander the ends of the earth for eternity," Asmodeus laughed.

But Gen couldn't be shaken. She felt a certainty in her spirit that the words she said were true. "No one is cut off from salvation, prince of fear. The blood atonement of Golgotha is for everyone."

Gen looked into Lucilius's hate-filled eyes.

"The Son of Man can set you free," she said.

Lucilius snarled and rushed at her so fast that neither Mark nor Myrddin could react in time, but he slammed into an invisible wall. It flashed red for a second, bouncing him back the way he had come, and became invisible again.

"Ah, a containment spell," Asmodeus said, walking to the barrier's edge. "And a very powerful one, too," he murmured with his hand reached out. There was a sizzling sound as sparks of electricity shot out between his hand and the invisible wall. "Indeed, a very powerful spell. But again, you underestimate me, young wizard. I am Asmodeus, and nothing on this earth can hold me."

He clenched his fist, and there was a loud bang as the containment field exploded.

9

Mark didn't hesitate as a man in a black suit rushed at him.

His Glock .45 rose swiftly, and he shot at the advancing attacker. The man staggered but continued charging. Mark aimed at his head and pulled the trigger, expecting the man to fall. The bullet's force threw the man's head back, but it barely slowed him down, and he snarled as he reached Mark and swung at his head.

Mark ducked under the fist and shoved his gun underneath the man's chin.

Let's see how you get out of this, he thought as he pulled the trigger.

The man fell to the ground. The man sprang back to his feet. There was no blood on his face; Mark's bullets hadn't penetrated his skin.

"We have a problem here," he shouted. "Bullets don't work on these guys."

The man brushed the dust off his suit and grinned maniacally. His face should have looked normal; it had eyes, a nose, and a mouth; but it lacked expression. The grin looked like a mannequin exposing its teeth. It was bizarre and uncanny.

Mark needed more firepower. He shoved his Glock .45 into his holster and swung up his MP7.

He saw another suited man try to sneak up on Myrddin and aimed. Bullets riddled the man's back, and he staggered away from the magician.

Mark's own opponent used the momentary distraction to slam his shoulder into him. Pain shot through Mark's chest; he felt as if a truck had run into him. The force of the impact bowled him over, and he tumbled backward.

The man in the black suit loomed over him, the same dead grin on his face as he raised his hand. Unusually long fingernails flew at Mark's face but stopped before making contact and burst into flames.

Mark turned to see Myrddin creating another ball of fire.

Myrddin grimaced as Asmodeus shattered his containment spell. His simulacra swarmed the ranch like angry wasps, and Gen stumbled backward as one rushed directly at her.

Myrddin blasted the man with a gust of focused air and sent him sailing back to the edge of the ranch. He needed to create another containment field. The noise of the attack could attract neighbours who may get caught in the crossfire. He spun his hand in a circle, and the air around it shimmered as spiritual essence shot out of him. Another black-suited assailant tried to grab his shirt, and Myrddin blasted that one back, too. His gust of air didn't seem to be hurting the men.

Asmodeus, Lucilius, and Remus hadn't moved. He must really believe that his doppelgängers can take care of everything, Myrddin thought.

His new containment spell snapped into place—a dome of shimmering light covering the ranch. He blasted another copy away from Gen, heard a grunt of pain, and turned to see Mark on the ground with one of Asmodeus's simulacra standing over him.

Myrddin dug deep into his emotions, and his anger flared. His fire responded and, like an eager child knowing it was finally allowed to play, it shook itself awake.

He aimed and released. Fire blossomed out of his hands and engulfed the man attacking Mark. There were no screams as fire reduced him to a heap of ash.

Myrddin became a raging inferno. He relished burning the simulacra away. Half of them were destroyed before Asmodeus decided to join the fray.

Gen's inner sight shone brightly. To her, the men rushing in looked like black spots, and she was glad to know they weren't living beings. She would have felt bad harming fellow humans, regardless of their affiliation or motivation. But with these, Gen wasn't planning on holding back.

She couldn't—or rather, wouldn't—use a gun, but she didn't plan on entering the fight defenceless. Doing so would have been an unnecessary burden and distraction to Mark. Gen had made him promise to look after himself, promising in return that she could fend for herself.

And she could.

A gust of wind drove back an approaching man. Her granddad's spell seemed to lack power because he rushed at her again, but the momentary break was enough for her to prepare.

She remembered the power flooding her when she brought Mark back from the dead. She tapped into that feeling, a mere fraction of what it was that night, and brought it to the forefront.

Gen's hands glowed white.

The man reached her and swung, and she leaned out of its path but stood firm. He missed, and she grabbed his shoulder as his fist sailed past her face.

Burn.

Bright light flared, and Gen squinted her eyes for a second. The man gave a wordless scream and burnt away, leaving charred specks floating in the air.

One down, many to go.

Josephine paced about the sitting room. She felt caged and useless. While she couldn't understand all that was going on, she thought she could be contributing to helping the people who seemed to have saved her life.

She couldn't keep running all her life.

"We have to do something," she said.

Isabella looked up from her phone. She was transcribing some of her recordings to see if she could come up with a good story. Whatever magic Gen's granddad did had made the world outside the windows invisible, leaving her relying only on audio.

"What can we do? You heard Gen. We'd be more of a nuisance than any help," Doctor O'Neal answered.

"So we just let them fight...alone?"

"Are they really doing anything? For all we know, they could just be standing there planning something nefarious."

"To what end? Why would they bother endangering themselves to save us from great peril and then plan to hurt us? It doesn't tally. I saw some weird stuff, and I'm inclined to believe them," she said.

"But how can we help?" came a voice from behind her.

Josephine had forgotten about Theo. The young officer had remained in the corner, keeping to himself.

"I don't know, but sitting here doing nothing sure isn't going to help."

Theo nodded.

Josephine was grateful someone felt the same way she did, and she strode out of the sitting room and walked to the front door with Theo trailing behind.

She reached for the door handle and paused.

Am I really doing this? Can I really help?

She took a deep breath, vaguely aware of Isabella shouting a warning behind her as she opened the door.

Mark scrambled to his feet and unsheathed his sword.

Guns and bullets were useless against these creatures; maybe a blade could cut their heads off. Balls of fire flew past as Myrddin laid waste to any man in a black suit hovering around him and Gen.

Mark was grateful. Even though he'd seen her obliterate one of the clones, he hated being this far from Gen.

One of Asmodeus's simulacra rushed toward him with that eerie silent scream of theirs. He spun, memories of combat flooding his mind and taking over his instinct. The sword bit into the doppelgänger's neck. He felt resistance, but the momentum carried through, and its head was lopped off.

There was a burst of black light, and Mark saw the spell that created the simulacrum disperse. The headless figure dissolved and vanished.

Mark grinned.

He was like an avenging angel. He spun and

swerved, dodging swinging arms and lunges. Black smoke burst around him as the simulacra died one after the other.

Josephine peered around from the front porch. The ranch was a war zone. Men in black suits were attacking Mark, Gen, and Gen's grandfather. Light erupted from Gen's hands and burned one of them into oblivion. Flames burst from Myrddin and engulfed them. Mark moved like death itself, his sword a giant scythe reaping the men in black suits. None challenged him and survived.

"Watch out!" Theo shouted, grabbing her from behind.

One of the black-suited men ran toward her and would have grabbed her if not for Theo's intervention.

They stumbled back into the house and fell into a pile on the floor just inside. The simulacrum crossed the house's threshold and burst into tiny black particles as it encountered Myrddin's spell.

"What the hell?" Theo said.

Josephine whooped with joy. "They can't get in," she said.

"I saw that."

"So we can bait them. I'll get their attention and lure them into the house."

"I don't think that's a good idea." O'Neal stood by the door leading to the sitting room with Isabella by his side.

"Listen to him, Josephine. You could get hurt."

Theo looked at Josephine and saw that she was determined to be useful. He nodded. He wanted to help too.

Josephine got to her feet, and they headed back to the door. She stepped out, not seeing the man in a black suit waiting for her. He grabbed her and flung her onto the porch.

"No!" Theo screamed. He pulled out his gun. The creature ignored Theo's repeated shots and reached for Josephine. His fingernails grew into sharp claws.

Josephine saw the hand coming down at her and tried to scramble to her feet. She wouldn't survive this, she thought sadly. It wasn't because she was about to be eviscerated; she was hurt because now she wouldn't be able to help Gen.

She wanted to be useful and felt there was a place for her here.

Her desire to live seemed to swell, and the air around her stirred. The clawed hand sweeping down seemed to stop in mid-air.

Josephine looked around in surprise. Everyone seemed to be frozen in place. She got to her feet and peered at the simulacrum before her. Its face was locked in a grotesque grin, and anger welled up within her. She pushed the man into the house as the world kicked back to normal.

The simulacrum burst apart.

Theo looked at her in amazement. "How did you get back here?" he smiled.

"It seems Gen was right—again. I can help her. I just need to catch my breath."

Josephine suddenly felt extremely tired. She resisted the urge to lie down; she had to help Gen and the others, so she sat on the floor in the corridor and leaned against the wall.

She decided to shut her eyes and rest—*just for a moment*. Her world went dark.

Mark clashed swords with Lucilius. The immortal joined the fight when it became apparent that Asmodeus's simulacra weren't going to win the day. Mark didn't mind. Lucilius was a familiar enemy. His movements were etched in Mark's mind, and he could see he now had the edge. Not that Lucilius was a pushover, but Mark had advanced. The visible flow of magic swirled around the immortal and allowed him to anticipate some of his intentions.

Lucilius aimed for his head, but Mark could tell it was a feint, and he stabbed forward instead. Lucilius narrowly avoided being skewered and danced back.

"The table's changed, Lucilius. Do you feel it?" Mark said.

Lucilius grunted and executed a flurry of moves that would have once incapacitated Mark, but now he saw through every move.

He prepared to strike again when he felt magic gathering in the distance.

The twang of an arrow leaving a bow was all Mark needed to hear. He swerved, and Remus's arrow sailed aimlessly away. Lucilius tried to use the distraction, but the tip of Mark's sword aimed at his throat dissuaded him.

Mark almost felt pity for Lucilius.

Almost.

"You can retreat. Leave this fight," Mark advised.

Lucilius snarled and rushed recklessly. Mark decided to end the fight when he felt a heavy pressure slam into him. Asmodeus made his presence known.

Asmodeus shot black energy at Myrddin, and it took all of his power to contain it. It was negative energy with the strength to erode anything it touched, unlike anything created in this plane of existence.

Asmodeus was revealing his real powers.

Myrddin looked sideways and saw Gen battling the two remaining simulacra. They had learned to be careful of Gen's glowing hands and tried to attack her from a distance.

He felt Asmodeus gathering another attack and reluctantly turned his attention back to his own battle. It wouldn't do the team any good if he was blasted by Asmodeus's death energy.

He willed his remaining affinities to manifest.

He created earth energy and caused the ground around Asmodeus to turn to mud. The demon sank to his ankles, and Myrddin solidified the earth, locking him in place. He quickly worked to freeze the air around him, hoping to trap Asmodeus in ice.

The plan worked for a mere few seconds before Asmodeus blasted the ice into a thousand pieces.

He broke out of the earth and advanced.

"Why do you come against me with mere party tricks, wizard? Do I look like a cur that you can beat with sticks? I am Asmodeus, prince of—"

Myrddin slammed a torrent of the hottest flames he could summon into Asmodeus.

Gen knew she could get close to the two remaining simulacra, but it would put her in striking distance, and she didn't want to find out what those claws of theirs could do.

She felt the fight between Myrddin and Asmodeus before she saw it. The air switched from icy cold to swelteringly hot as they battled. But despite his efforts, she could see nothing seemed to hold the demon, and she grew worried.

An idea came to her, and she summoned the light within her again. She allowed the power to flood out of her, but this time she interrupted the flow. A shard of light shot out of her hands and pierced the two men in black suits.

The doppelgängers twitched in wordless agony before bursting into pieces.

Gen didn't wait; she didn't hesitate. She turned to Asmodeus and released all the power she could at him.

The whole ranch flared brightly as her power tested the strength of Myrddin's containment shield. Her essence slammed into Asmodeus. He bellowed in pain and anger as the light washed over him.

Lucilius flinched as the end of Gen's power washed over him. There was a sharp burning pain, and blisters formed on his arm. He felt defenceless and was surprised to see that Mark didn't take advantage of his moment of weakness.

The bright light ended as quickly as it was summoned, and Lucilius felt his body start its healing process, albeit very slowly. He knew if he had been caught in the centre of the blast, it would have been the end of him. For a fraction of a second, he wondered if that would have been such a bad thing.

Gen staggered back, almost slumping if not for Myrddin's hold on her arm. She waited with bated breath as the mist that formed in the shadow of her powers dissipated.

Asmodeus's face was a grotesque mask of pain and agony. His flesh rippled as the raw, exposed flesh tried to heal and failed. He opened his eyes and looked in Gen's direction.

"I will flay you like a rabbit while you watch. I will dismember everyone here before your eyes, Nail Bearer."

His flesh knitted back together, and he slammed everyone with his power.

Gen knew it wasn't real, but she couldn't stop the anguish that tore at her heart. She was in a motel room. Blood was splattered everywhere. Her parents' lifeless eyes stared at her accusingly. They were twisted into a vile position that showed their killer had dredged up some sick fantasies in their demise.

"I'm so sorry, Mum. I'm so sorry."

She was a failure. How could she save the world if she couldn't even save her parents?

Myrddin felt every death. He was the cause of this misery—a bringer of death. He walked slowly through the carnage and destruction he had caused. He wished he could take this day back, but that was impossible. Despite all his abilities, he couldn't time travel. His past mistakes would remain forever.

What would Gen think of him if she knew of my past?

Would she still smile with admiration and love at him if she could see this part of his mind? Myrddin knew he was a failure.

Mark was back in Afghanistan.

His Special Forces jacket ruffled as the air around him was displaced by the rotors of the approaching helicopter.

The mission had been a complete failure. The intel was false, and they had walked into friendly fire. In the quick and brutal exchange, instinct had taken over, and Mark was the only survivor.

They would brand him a hero, but Mark knew the truth. He had killed his fellow soldiers—people who had been in the wrong place at the wrong time.

One of the victims had been a young man, little more than a kid. It was only his first tour, and now he would return in a body bag.

The young man had died at his hands, brought down by his bullets.

Mark had failed that day.

But he had atoned. He visited the young man's ailing mother and begged her for forgiveness. That was the incident that made him retire from the army. His past didn't burden him. The soldier's mother forgave him, understanding the circumstances involved.

She refused his attempt to help with the funeral bills but hadn't stopped him from opening a trust fund for her grandchild.

Mark was free from his past. He shook off Asmodeus's hold on his mind and advanced, his sword gripped by his side.

Mark almost ended the fight in a single blow. Asmodeus didn't expect anyone would break his hold, so Mark had gotten close to him. He swung his sword, and the prince of hell managed to dodge just in time. Mark followed with a straight lunge, but Asmodeus willed a sword of black energy into existence and deflected the attempt.

"How are you able to break free?"

"I've come to terms with my past. I have been forgiven."

Mark could see that Asmodeus was much stronger than Lucilius or anybody he had ever fought, but that didn't stop him. He needed to end the fight quickly.

He lunged at Asmodeus and, in an explosive exchange, cut in vital spots.

He groaned. Asmodeus didn't need to heal. None of Mark's blows even broke the demon's skin.

Asmodeus went on the offensive, and Mark had to retreat. While the demon could afford to be hit by Mark, Mark couldn't allow himself to be touched by his negative energy sword.

He dredged up all the memories he could as he dodged and deflected Asmodeus's swings. The inevitable occurred some minutes into the fight as Mark swung, and Asmodeus brought up his own sword to block the strike: Mark's sword snapped in two.

Mark didn't stop.

He used the momentum to jump at Asmodeus and grab him in a scissor hold. The force allowed him to flip the demon over, and they both landed on the floor.

Gen felt Asmodeus's grip on her mind break. She looked around to see Mark pummelling him with punches. The blows didn't seem to bother Asmodeus, and he sprang to his feet and grabbed Mark by the neck.

She didn't wait for Asmodeus to complete his move. She ran and grabbed the hand on Mark's throat.

"Burn."

Gen released all she had left. Another blast of white light slammed into Asmodeus, and the prince screamed in agony. She shouted in defiance as she continued to pour everything she had into burning the demon out of existence.

She staggered and almost fell as the hand she had been holding disappeared. She looked around in confusion.

Asmodeus had fled. They had won—at least for now.

Gen slumped to the ground, feeling empty and drained.

Mark slid down beside her. They supported each other, and she could see he was close to passing out.

"Took your time in coming up with that," he said, smiling.

Gen chuckled and grimaced as she felt the start of a headache. "Didn't want to visit the hospital again so soon."

"They'd probably drive us out this time. Especially after all the commotion you caused the last time."

Gen heard her granddad approaching, and she looked up. He still had that look of sadness and regret, and Gen promised herself she would talk to her granddad soon.

"Guess what they left behind?" he said.

Myrddin held up a nail, and Mark began to laugh but was cut short as the air stirred around them and burst with light. Mark tried to get to his feet, but Gen held him down.

She knew who was coming.

A figure stepped out of the ripple he had formed in space.

"Baraqiel."

Gen acknowledged the angel's presence with a nod.

"You know, we could have used your help like thirty minutes ago," Mark said, shielding his eyes from Baraqiel's face.

"You had the situation well in hand," he rumbled.

Mark felt the soil beneath his hands vibrate. He felt light-headed and had to quell the feeling he might pass out.

"Why are you here, Baraqiel?" Myrddin asked.

The angel looked into the distance and pointed west of the ranch. "The time has come to bring all three nails together."

Gen, Mark, and Myrddin stared.

We only just got the second nail, Mark thought.

Did Baraqiel know? Were angels limited in how they interacted with humanity? Mark had a thousand questions he wished he could ask.

157

What rank of angels was Baraqiel?

"That which you seek will come into this town tomorrow. Be at the baker's before noon. Bring the one called Theo."

"Why do we have to bring Theo?" Gen wondered.

"His decision will affect humanity."

Gen was shocked. She hadn't wanted Theo involved in her fight against the accursed, but it seemed he was destined to be part of it.

"We will get the last nail tomorrow?" Gen asked.

"If you follow my instructions," Baraqiel said, then turned to Myrddin. "You must use your anvil one more time and make the protector the sword he needs to fight the approaching darkness."

Baraqiel vanished, casting the ranch in shadows.

Mark fell back to the ground and closed his eyes.

10

CONSTANTINOPLE, 327 A.D.

A long line formed as people in hooded robes queued up to get into the compound. Merlin watched from among the crowd as those in the front of the line whispered the password to the guards at the gate.

It was the early hours of the day, and the area was still. Even the occasional barking of restless dogs didn't disturb the sleeping city.

Merlin wondered if a spell was in effect to keep it this quiet, but he hadn't sensed anything when he had joined the line of people approaching the compound. The building inside was a broken-down bungalow that had once belonged to Emperor Constantine's late son, Crispus.

The irony of the situation didn't escape Merlin, as there were rumours that Constantine had his son executed for treason.

Merlin whispered a spell, and the air around the gate filtered the sound back to him.

"They say Hyginos will speak tonight," a female voice said with reverence.

"It is time for change in this city."

"I hope they serve food. I didn't get to eat anything before coming here."

"Hope my sister doesn't see me here."

The words filtered into Merlin's hearing, and he sorted through them. He approached the gate, and the guards stared at the couple standing in front of him.

"Maximian shall rise again!" the man said.

Merlin watched the guards part for the couple to pass through the gate, and his turn came.

"Maximian shall rise again," he whispered. He prepared a spell as one of the guards tried to peer under his hood, but the other guards looked around in boredom and waved for him to move along. He glanced back at the throng of people waiting to get into the compound. Calisto and some palace guards were in the crowd, waiting for his signal.

Merlin had returned to the tavern where he had overheard the conversation with the two men. It had taken some time, but they had eventually returned.

From there, he followed them to their hideout, where he heard about this meeting. He'd informed Queen Helena, and a detachment of palace guards was waiting to round up the insurgents.

Maybe everything will end tonight.

He followed the crowd through a narrow passageway into what looked like it was once a mini-amphitheatre.

The crowd gathered, the air thick with tension as they waited for their summoner to appear.

They didn't have long to wait long.

A man in his late thirties strode to the platform and was greeted with cheers and applause.

"Hyginos, Hyginos, Hyginos," they chanted.

Merlin realized he could sense the tinge of magic at a low level. The crowd wasn't being controlled, but their emotions were being heightened. They could be whipped into a frenzy without anyone noticing the subtle manipulation.

The man on the platform beckoned for them to quiet down, and they obeyed.

"My fellow brethren," he started.

Merlin and Calisto agreed the man before him could only be Remus.

"We are here because we are worried. Worried for our children, our wives, and our mothers. Worried for our sons and our fathers who will have to bear the brunt of this government. For the emperor does not care for you and me."

The imposter's words ignited murmurs of agreement and nodding of heads.

"Emperor Constantine burdens us with taxes while he builds luxurious palaces and gets fat on our sweat. We toil day and night only to be left with little to feed and cater to our loved ones. Well, enough is enough. We are the people, and we have a voice."

The imposter pumped his fist, and the magic in the air intensified. The crowd screamed in agreement and bellowed in approval.

Blood would spill tonight if Merlin couldn't find a way to stop the accursed.

Calisto heard the roar of the crowd and signalled for his soldiers to stop. They were some meters away from the compound and saw the guards stationed at the gate.

He felt bad for the guards. They were probably doing their duty for a member of the senate, but that didn't stop him from giving the go-ahead.

Javelins whistled through the air, and the guards staggered. Some clutched their throats as they were pierced, while others grunted and collapsed.

With Helena's personal guards, Calisto rushed to the gate and quickly removed the bodies of the slain guards. They stood and listened, and when Calisto was certain their presence hadn't been detected, he called for the cohort to advance.

The soldiers jogged silently into the compound in unison and quickly surrounded the amphitheatre's entrance.

Calisto stood with his men and waited for Merlin's signal.

It would end tonight.

Merlin looked around. Atticus had to be around somewhere. Magic crackled in the air, and the crowd continued to roar in support of Hyginos. They were riled up, and Merlin knew the tiniest spark could set them off.

He shoved people aside as he moved in the direction of the spell's origin.

There.

Atticus stood beside a pillar close to the platform. Just out of sight of the crowd, his hands moved rapidly, forming the glyphs necessary to ignite his spell.

"That is enough."

Merlin's voice carried across with authority, and Atticus froze.

The crowd fell silent. Merlin knew that he had mere seconds before it was too late. The hooded people around him stared from the shrouded darkness that was their faces.

"Ah, Merlin, the interloper. Unfortunately, you can see that you're too late." Atticus waved his hand to indicate the crowd.

"The spell's not done, Atticus. It's still missing its focus. And you know I won't let you achieve that."

"Oh, I know, Merlin. That's why we came prepared."

Merlin frowned. If Atticus wasn't planning on finishing the spell, it needed someone else with magic to set it off.

Someone like–

"Hear me!"

The words rang with enough power that, for a second, Merlin felt himself obeying. He shook off the feeling with a flick of his finger.

163

Another individual joined the imposter at the platform, and Merlin understood the nature of their plan.

While Atticus created the spell, Marius was the catalyst. His words carried power, but he didn't have the strength for magic of this magnitude. Neither Marius nor Atticus could achieve it individually, but they did something better—they shared their powers. Atticus bore the load while Marius rode the spell, so to speak.

The crowd stood transfixed, waiting for Marius's next words.

Merlin had no intention of letting that happen.

Though sharing the burden was an excellent plan, it had one major disadvantage—disrupting either Atticus or Marius's hold was enough to shatter it.

Merlin gathered his energy to attack when one of the robed figures nearby burst into motion. The figure moved in a blur, and Merlin tried to step sideways.

The figure pulled a sword from a sheath and struck. It was perfectly executed, and Merlin knew he wouldn't be able to avoid the blow.

It struck Merlin's magical shield, which flared a vivid blue. He created a pillar of air and blasted the figure with it in response. The assailant grunted, and the force of the blast shoved him back, knocking back his hood as he slid across the sand.

"Good of you to show your face, Lucilius. I'm glad you didn't make it difficult to track you lot down."

Merlin thanked God he didn't have to fight all four immortals tonight.

Atticus and Marius would have to concentrate on the spell and wouldn't have time to engage him. That left Lucilius and Remus.

Not that it would be easy, just not impossible.

Lucilius blurred again, and Merlin felt another blow strike his shield. He shot streams of condensed air back, and the immortal deflected and dodged them. Merlin used the momentary reprieve to aim at Atticus. The gust of air slammed into a shield, and Atticus flinched at the attack, but his shield held.

Another flare of blue brought Merlin's attention back to Lucilius. He grunted in annoyance.

He needed help.

The amphitheatre had become unusually quiet, and Calisto sensed something was wrong. Merlin suggested he go in alone, and Calisto knew he could handle himself, but no one was invincible.

Calisto saw a flare of light and turned to his men.

"Get ready to move. Remember, shield formation. Most of the people here are civilians but protect yourselves if you need to."

They moved in. Calisto immediately noted the number of people as his men spread out to cover the back of the amphitheatre.

The crowd didn't stir, and Calisto frowned. Merlin warned him the accursed could be here, and he suspected foul magic was at play. He heard the sound of combat near the platform and turned to his second-in-command.

"Form a shield wall. Make sure no one escapes and be careful. There are men here who are more than they seem."

His second-in-command nodded. He had been with Calisto when they had brought Queen Helena back to Constantinople. He had encountered Marius and had lived to tell the tale. Calisto signalled to every man in the cohort to place a little wax in their ears. From now on, they would communicate through hand signals.

Calisto gripped his second-in-command by the shoulder and nodded, then advanced toward the platform, weaving through the crowd. They didn't stop his advance, and within moments, Calisto saw Merlin shooting streams of compressed air at Lucilius.

They both saw Calisto at the same time.

"Stop Marius!" Merlin shouted.

Marius was on the platform with the man they suspected was Remus. Marius strained against an invisible force and then inhaled deeply.

"People of Constantinople. BURN THE CITY DOWN."

Calisto felt the power of Marius's words wash over him but shrugged it off.

The crowd turned as a single entity and faced the soldiers blocking their way. Calisto knew they were about to witness a bloodbath of unprecedented proportions.

The crowd began to respond to Marius's words instantly. Merlin knew he had less than a second before blood was spilled. Creating a vortex spell, he blasted Lucilius, and everything in his radius, away. He quickly channelled his essence again and slammed a containment shield in place, separating the crowd from the soldiers.

The mob slammed into the containment field, and Merlin grunted as he bore the weight of more than a thousand people. He saw Lucilius get up from the dirt and glare at him. Calisto hurried to Merlin's side and aimed his sword at the immortal.

"Now, what do we do?" he asked.

"I need a moment to work something out," Merlin panted. The push of bodies on the containment field was wearing on him. He could only watch as Calisto stepped forward to engage Lucilius in battle, the sound of clashing swords vibrating through the air.

Merlin had a plan but needed a little time to execute it. His hands moved swiftly, forming sigils in the air and imbibing the sigils with power. Merlin watched Calisto spin and cut Lucilius across the chest, who took the hit without showing any sign of pain and kicked Calisto in the stomach. The force knocked Calisto backward, and Lucilius advanced on him.

The accursed swung his sword, and Merlin stomped his foot on the ground. A chunk of earth rose shot at Lucilius and made his strike miss its target.

Merlin clapped his hands together when the spell clicked, and power flooded into him. His eyes shone bright, and he felt the strength of a hundred men fill him.

The power would only last for a single spell.

"SLEEP," Merlin bellowed.

He had created a copy of Marius's power and could only use it for a moment.

It would be enough.

Everybody in the amphitheatre slumped to the ground as the spell hit them. Calisto and the accursed staggered to their knees as they fought the workings of the spell. Calisto tried to remain awake but fell face-first on the sand.

Merlin walked toward the accursed and tried to create a lance of compressed air, but the shape wouldn't solidify. The spell needed more energy than he had left.

"It seems you get to live," he said.

Merlin could see the strain that resisting his spell was having on them. They struggled to their feet and staggered away. He watched them go, not enough strength remaining to do anything else. The spell had weakened him, too. Merlin let out a deep lung-ful of air and leaned against the raised platform.

It would be unbecoming to pass out now.

11

Mark felt the rays of the early morning sun on his face and opened his eyes.

They had survived.

He looked around. He and Gen had managed to drag themselves to the sitting room and had fallen to the floor. By general consensus, everybody decided to pass the night here, too. The ladies took the sofas while the men slept on the floor.

Mark slowly got to his feet and stretched. They had a busy day ahead of them, and the sooner they prepared, the better his focus would be. He felt the tiny tug of magic and saw Myrddin meditating behind one of the sofas, legs crossed and his palms resting on his knees.

"Don't tell me you were in that position all night," Mark grumbled. He could feel his joints aching just imagining himself in Myrddin's pose.

"It is relaxing, and it helps me replenish lost essence," Myrddin said gently.

169

Mark wondered for a moment how he had known Myrddin was awake. He saw Gen open her eyes and smile at him and the feelings she had for him poured through the space between them.

"What time is it?" she asked.

Mark looked at his wristwatch. "Six thirty-five."

Gen groaned as she sat up.

"We may have a busy day ahead of us, so it would be wise to be up and about," Myrddin said with his eyes still closed.

Mark felt the rest of the occupants start to stir.

An hour later, bathed and feeling better after break-fast, Gen dusted the breadcrumbs off her shirt and turned to her granddad.

The sitting room was crammed with everyone present at once. Mark had suggested meeting in the kitchen, but Gen believed they all had a right to know what was happening. She was glad when she heard about Josephine's contribution to the fight. They had been right, and Gen was grateful for the help the teacher had offered.

"So, I'm guessing Baraqiel meant Mrs. Mayfield's. Right, Granddad?"

"That would be correct."

"And we're sure hers is the only bakery in town?" Mark added.

"Yes. The only shop that comes close to being a bakery, anyway. It's mostly a meeting point for the occasional meeting and bingo," Gen explained. She resisted smiling when she saw Isabella raise her hand.

"You don't have to be so formal, Isabella," Gen said.

Isabella nodded. "An actual angel was here last night? And the angel wants us to meet in a bakery?" O'Neal snorted. Gen wondered what his abilities were and how he would respond when they manifested. She also hoped it would be sooner rather than later.

"We've gone through this before, Isabella, and with what you've seen, believing in the existence of angels shouldn't be so farfetched," Myrddin said.

"That's the thing. I was stuck in here last night. I didn't witness anything. Didn't even hear noises, well, except when Lara Croft here decided to open the front door, but that could have been anything."

O'Neal nodded in agreement, and Theo frowned. He opened his mouth to say something but then decided to keep quiet.

"Everything Gen said is real. You want an eyewitness account? Well, I was there," Josephine said. Her confidence and boldness seemed to have increased since the night before.

"But did you see the angel?" O'Neal questioned. He waited for Josephine's answer and smiled in triumph when she shook her head.

"It's real."

Gen was surprised to hear Theo speak. He shifted uncomfortably when he noticed that all eyes were on him.

"I couldn't remain inside doing nothing, especially after Josephine here went outside." He stopped and glanced over at Josephine before continuing. "I waited till the noise died down and then snuck outside," He laughed ruefully.

"I'd never been more scared in my life. There was someone on the ranch. I couldn't make out the features, but the shape looked human. There was a bright light around the being that was impossible to see through. If that wasn't an angel…" Theo trailed off, but his words had profoundly affected everyone.

Myrddin broke the silence and got to his feet.

"Regardless of what anyone believes, we have a job to do. We don't know who or what we'll be meeting. The message was simple, and it would be prudent to prepare."

"I propose Gen, Myrddin, Theo, and I head to town. The rest of you will be safe as long as you remain in the house," Mark stated.

"I'm going," Isabella said, and Mark shook his head.

"We don't know what we'll be walking into. It would be safer if—"

"Unless you plan on tying me to a bed, I'm coming along. Anyway, as the designated PR of this merry band, I need to be where the action is."

Mark raised an eyebrow, and Gen hid a smile.

"I'm coming too." Josephine smiled sheepishly and shrugged when Mark tried to stare her down. "I can help," she added.

Mark turned to O'Neal. "That means you're coming along, too."

They couldn't leave the doctor behind, so he might as well tag along. At least that way, Mark could keep an eye on him. O'Neal grunted in acceptance.

"Need to get some stuff anyway. Don't imagine wearing the same clothes is hygienic."

It was a silent trip into town. Mark drove Gen, Josephine, and Isabella. The reporter seemed serious about sticking to Gen like glue, but if Gen wasn't complaining, Mark was good.

The rest of the group followed in Myrddin's van. They stopped at the police station and parked. Mark immediately noticed the stares from the residents as their group walked toward the bakery.

Mark looked at his watch.

Ten forty-five.

They were early, but Mark was okay with that. He needed the time to plot out escape routes and potential choke points they could use if things went south.

The police station only had one way in and out, so it would be a death trap. Mark didn't know the layout of many other buildings in town, so he decided against making a stand inside one.

They would remain in the open, where they had multiple paths of escape.

Gen tried to ignore the stares their group was getting. She knew people meant well and probably weren't used to seeing this many strange faces in one day. Dundurn never got visitors, so seeing the doctor, Isabella, and Josephine might make the residents curious.

"What do we do now?" Gen said. They were early.

Her granddad shrugged. "You heard what Baraqiel said. We have to be here before noon. And bring him along." Myrddin tipped his head toward Theo, who stood by the van trying to look inconspicuous. "So we'll just have to wait and see," he concluded.

Laughter from inside Mrs. Mayfield's bakery drew the group's attention. They watched as an elderly couple walked out, and Gen recognized Mrs. Mayfield immediately, but the elderly man at her side was a mystery.

The couple stopped by the door when they saw the group walk toward them. Mrs. Mayfield was in her eighties, and she had a weather-beaten face with laugh lines around her eyes. Her hands shook slightly as she held the shop keys in her hands.

"There's nothing to be alarmed about, Mrs. Mayfield," Myrddin said reassuringly.

"Oh, my goodness. How may we help you all? Unfortunately, the bakery won't be open until tomorrow," she said.

"That's okay, Mrs. Mayfield." Gen stepped forward to see if she would recognize her and was glad to see a flicker of recognition in her eyes.

"Is that you, Genesis Isherwood?"

"Yes, Mrs. Mayfield."

"Heard you came back to stay at the ranch. Oh, but you look different. And why do you have sunglasses on?"

"Doctor's prescription, Mrs. Mayfield."

Gen beckoned Theo over, and he reluctantly walked over. Baraqiel had said Theo needed to be present in this meeting.

"Good day, Mrs. Mayfield," Theo greeted.

"Ah, Theo. Good to see you."

Gen saw Mrs. Mayfield relax. She turned to the man beside her.

"Don't you remember young Theo Cuttaham, Adam?"

The elderly man squinted in Theo's direction.

"Theo? Theo Cuttaham, Liam's kid? Is that really you, boy?" He walked to Theo and patted Theo on the head. "You little rascal. Always chasing after old Billy, the goat."

"That's your great-grandson, Adam. Theo is Liam's boy. Used to follow you to Saskatoon them summers."

"Ah, Theo, Theo. It's been ages since I last saw you." Adam folded Theo in a hug, his fragile body gently pressed against him. "You used to love bringing strange things to the house, saying they were treasures. Couldn't get rid of you. Did you ever find anything interesting?"

"No, Mr. Elliot," Theo said with a red face.

"Well, I have something you'll find interesting. Bought it a year ago at an auction in Spain when

175

I travelled to see my grandchildren. Said to bring good luck. All you have to do is nail it to your door-post. Who knows, maybe you'll get the girl of your dreams or such."

Theo turned a deeper shade of crimson, but no one in the group paid him any attention. All eyes were on Adam as he dug into a small bag by his side and produced a nail.

Gen heard Myrddin inhale. She could feel the nail's faint pull, and she wondered if it was the last piece they needed.

It was rusty and chipped at its hexagonal sides. For a moment, nobody moved; they all stared in shock at the nail in Mr. Elliot's wrinkled hand.

"Theo?" Mr. Elliot said with a puzzled expression.

"Eh, this looks interesting, Mr. Elliot." Theo's hand shook slightly as he reached out and took the nail.

"Funny thing is, I was thinking of you when I bought the thing. Remembered how you used to bring me scraps and bits from God knows where. Stayed more at my house than you did at yours," Mr. Elliot laughed.

"Can...eh, can...I keep it?" Theo asked.

Gen held her breath. Mr. Elliot looked at the nail in his hand and then at Theo.

"Boy, I don't really need a good luck charm at my age. Maybe it could be of use to you," he said.

Gen couldn't believe her eyes. They had shed blood for the foot nail in her possession. The accursed had hunted and hounded them. And here was one being handed to them just like that—just as Baraqiel had said.

She barely heard the rest of the conversation.

We have the three nails in our possession.

For the first time in over a thousand years, the nails were together in the hands of the nail bearer.

Gen felt overwhelmed. She remained watched in a daze the whole drive back to the ranch.

Mark resisted the urge to drum his fingers on the steering wheel. He felt good. For once, the day went by without any nasty surprises or the need to survive a bloody fight.

He had half-expected Asmodeus to spring into their midst and snatch the nail out of Mr. Elliot's hand or Lucilius to pop out of thin air and stab the old man in the chest.

Mark was very glad to be proven wrong.

No blood was shed. They had the three nails, and from the look of joy on Myrddin's face, he knew it was a good thing.

He was so deep in thought that he almost didn't see the man standing by the Triple 7 gates. He slammed the brakes just in time, and the car screeched to a halt. Myrddin's van bumped into him from behind.

Mark stared at the familiar figure blocking the gate. He wasn't surprised. He knew the day couldn't end on a peaceful note.

Not after they'd been given this treasure.

He opened the car door and stepped out. Gen followed immediately.

Looking as though he didn't have a care in the world, Lucilius stood in the middle of the road.

Mark wasn't fooled. He could see the beads of sweat trailing down the sides of Lucilius's face. The look in the immortal's eyes was one of resignation.

Mark scanned the area. He dug deep into his ability to sense any presence, but his worries weren't eased when he came up with nothing.

"He's alone," he told Gen.

He didn't need to turn to know who was walking up to them from behind. Mark could feel the power gathering of power as Myrddin prepared a spell against Lucilius.

Gen was surprised to see Lucilius. He stood leaning against the gate as though the combined might of Gen, her granddad, and Mark didn't amount to anything to be worried over.

He tracked her with his eyes as she stopped beside Mark and watched Lucilius.

If he thought he could surprise us, he's doing a terrible job.

"Is it possible?" Lucilius asked.

Gen was taken aback. She knew what Lucilius was asking about. She had told him during the fight, and she believed it.

"It's possible," she replied firmly.

"What would you have me do?"

12

I don't trust him."

Mark leaned by the kitchen window and stared at Lucilius, who remained by the ranch's gate. He, Gen, and Myrddin had left the rest of the group in the sitting room while they conferred in the kitchen.

"He has to be up to something. It must be a trap," Mark insisted.

"Why do you think so?" Gen asked.

He shook his head and pointed in Lucilius's direction with both hands.

"Because it's Lucilius! The accursed. One of the immortals who has been after the nails. I refuse to believe that it's a mere coincidence that the moment we acquire all three nails, Lucilius appears and wants to be all buddy-buddy. I don't buy it."

Gen tapped the kitchen table as she tried to think.

Could Lucilius really want to change? Can he change? And could the darkness within him be purged?

He who the Son sets free is free indeed.

The words kept resounding in her spirit—the exact words she had told Lucilius last night.

"I think he wants to be free," she uttered.

Mark shook his head in exasperation and turned to Myrddin.

"Will you make her see reason? She has to accept that some people can't be changed. Some people have sold out to evil. That's why we're where we are today. Lucilius can't be changed."

"Who are we to decide who can or cannot be changed?" Myrddin asked softly. "I never thought I could be changed, and yet, here I am."

"That's different," Mark said.

"How so?" Myrddin asked and looked up from his seat at Mark.

"It just is. We may all have done something we're ashamed of, or there may be an evil act so terrible in our past…" Mark noticed Myrddin wince at his statement. "But that doesn't make us evil. In this case, ignorance actually makes us excusable. Lucilius's case is different. He knowingly chose this path. He sold his soul to gain this power. He is not redeemable."

Gen frowned. Mark's reasoning made sense. And yet, the words kept ringing in her soul.

"What if God's involved in this?"

Mark looked in her direction with a frown on his face. Even Myrddin seemed questioning, but Gen's instinct told her she was on the right path.

"What if God, deciding to show the magnitude of His mercy and grace, chooses to forgive Lucilius? To make him an example of the fact that He can choose anyone and change anyone?"

Gen saw Mark open his mouth to counter her statement. She quickly added, "As long as they genuinely want to change. I think that's the deciding factor here. If Lucilius genuinely wants to change, he can change."

"But does he really want to change, or is all this a ploy to allow him into our midst?" Mark said, staring into Gen's eyes, imploring her to reconsider.

"I think all this is moot if Gen can't do her part," Myrddin said.

Again, Gen felt the weight of both Mark and her granddad's eyes on her.

Was it possible? Gen remembered her granddad telling her stories from the bible. Paul was changed when he had an encounter with the Messiah. And what was her part in all this? She didn't have the power to change anyone – but she could point him at the cross. Lucilius needed to have an encounter; like she did. Like her grandfather had at some point in his life. But how did she go about telling someone like Lucilius of a better way? Had it even been done before? Had Queen Helena done anything like what she was attempting?

'Do you know if Queen Helena tried anything like this?' Gen asked her granddad.

'Not that I know of.' Myrddin stated.

"Even if it is successful, what do we do then? Welcome him with a pat on the back and tell him that everything's all right?" Mark asked. He couldn't accept that Lucilius could change. If that could happen, then what had they been fighting for? What was he fighting for?

"If Gen or I were to change to a version you felt was wrong, would you go to any length to try and get us back?" Myrddin said.

Mark gritted his teeth. He knew where the line of questioning was heading.

"You know I would. But Lucilius isn't a friend or a brother."

"But he could be," Gen said softly.

"Yeah, right. Maybe in two lifetimes. My eyes will always be on Lucilius, and my hand always on my gun."

"We wouldn't expect anything less," Myrddin chuckled. His expression sobered up when he saw the worry on Gen's face. "You've been moving by your instincts all this while. Trust yourself," he encouraged her.

Gen still wasn't sure of the next move, but a plan slowly crept into her mind. She remembered the incident at the hospital. Atticus came against her with dark, negative powers, and she had been able to blow the powers away. Maybe she could try burning the darkness within Lucilius away.

Would that even work?

"If you're really going to do this, we might as well do it right," Mark sighed in resignation. If what he had in mind was a fraction of what was going to happen, his expertise was needed. "I can't do the whole bright light thing, but I have a feeling we'll need to restrain him. We're going to need an immovable chair…" Mark looked toward Myrddin, who nodded. "I don't know if we need to restrain him physically or if magic would be better. Again, I'll bow to your knowledge in that matter, Myrddin. Who'll do the…eh…exorcism?"

"I don't think exorcism is the right word," Gen said.

"… well, whatever you want to call it goes. We'll need to do it somewhere isolated and controlled. I'll suggest the barn. If he goes all Lucilius on us, nobody has to see the mess he'll end up in."

"All Lucilius?" Gen asked with a smirk.

"Knowing who he is, I'll take that as a yardstick for degrees of craziness."

Though Mark made light of the situation, Gen could see he was deadly serious. He would end Lucilius's life if it came to that. She only hoped that it wouldn't get to that stage. Lucilius may be vile and evil, but she didn't want his death on her conscience.

Killing him in a heated battle was one thing; strapping him to a chair and having Mark end his life for a mistake she made was another.

Gen took a deep breath and got to her feet. "I don't think delaying this will bring any other solution."

Mark took a chair to the barn and set it in the middle of the open space some meters away from Myrddin's workplace. He brought Lucilius to the barn next. He stood in a corner, watching Myrddin hold the chair's arms and whisper spells.

The earth around the chair softened, and it sank a couple of inches into the ground. Myrddin released the magic, and it hardened again. He ran his palm gently along the chair's surface. Mark couldn't see the spell, but he felt it strengthening the chair.

Myrddin stood straight when he was done and nodded to Gen.

"Your white hair and beard make me forget who you are," Mark said with a shake of his head. Myrddin might have the smiling face of a doting granddad, but he was anything but weak.

Mark noticed Lucilius eyeing the enchanted chair suspiciously. "You know you can still back out now. I'll even allow you out of the ranch just to show you I can be nice," he said.

"You are a man without honour. You fight without honour. Why should I trust any word you say?"

"You talk about honour but have the audacity to heal any wound you receive. At least I won't stab you in the back in a fight."

"Boys, that's enough," Gen chided. Mark was making her nervous, and her fear of failure was bubbling to the surface. Mark spotted the look on her face and nodded, indicating he was willing to back down from any confrontation with Lucilius.

"I take it I'm to sit on there while you do whatever you need to do?"

Gen nodded and indicated for Lucilius to sit down. He walked boldly to the chair and sat down, but Mark spotted the flash of fear that flickered across his face.

Myrddin waved his hand over Lucilius's, and bands of air wrapped around his hands, binding him to the chair.

"Before we do this, now may be a good time to interrogate him," Mark stated. Lucilius snapped his head up and glared at Mark.

"I knew you were without honour. Only a coward would do what you're planning."

"Only a fool would overlook what I'm planning," Mark countered.

"What are you doing, Mark?" Gen asked with a frown. She didn't know what Mark was up to, but she wouldn't allow him to torture Lucilius.

Mark shook his head in annoyance. "Give me some credit, will you? If I did what both of you think I'm about to do, it would only make me like him. Yes, I'm angry, and I have every right to be. The asshole sitting right here stabbed me. Twice. They must have been thinking of him when they coined the word backstabber. I have no plans of torturing him; I just need a few questions answered."

"And if I refuse to speak?" Lucilius snarled.

"Wouldn't faze me one bit. Just thought I'd get some answers in case...you know... you don't make it through this whole...process."

Everyone was silent until Lucilius barked, "Ask your question."

"Where is Remus?"

"I don't know."

"What do you mean you don't know? I know the guy's a coward, but I thought you were the leader of the gang?"

"I do not know his whereabouts. We parted ways after the fight last night. I met him this morning and asked him to join me in coming here, but he refused."

"Why?"

"I don't know. He chose to go to Asmodeus. I didn't want anything to do with the demon."

"Because you don't like being anyone's lapdog. Your pride couldn't allow it," Mark uttered. Lucilius remained silent, refusing to rise to Mark's baiting.

"And talking about Asmodeus, what has he got planned for us?"

"Very bad things."

"Can you be a little more specific than that?"

"Asmodeus has never had to retreat from a foe before. He will definitely attack here with a greater force."

"And you know this because…?"

"Because that's what I'd do. I'd come back and crush you all, even if I had to empty hell itself."

Gen shivered. She had decided not to interrupt Mark when she realized he was doing what no one else would have thought of—gathering information on the enemy. Gen knew information was crucial to any fight.

Mark indicated he was done, and Gen took a deep breath.

Now or never.

She didn't know what else to do, so she made her hand glow with her power and reached out to Lucilius. He flinched, but he had nowhere to run.

She placed her hand on Lucilius's arm, and he screamed in anguish as the world shifted on its axis.

"What have you done to me? Is this how you intend to save my soul, woman?"

"Be quiet!"

Gen ignored Lucilius and looked around. It was night. There was a rumbling, and the earth shook. The air was heavy, lightning shattered the dark at intervals, and Gen heard the gasps of awe and fear from scared lips.

"Indeed, he was the Son of God."

Gen turned to see a centurion standing and looking up at the cross in awe.

They were back at Golgotha.

Lucilius walked to the centurion and waved his hand in front of his face.

"Don't bother. They can't see us. We're here to learn something."

"Learn what? This is where the Nazarene was crucified. What can be learnt from here?"

Gen was a bit surprised Lucilius knew where they were, but then, he had played an active role in the circumstances leading to Jesus's crucifixion.

"We're here for you, Lucilius. Your beginnings."

The words seemed appropriate, and Gen followed with her instincts. Lucilius grunted. The rumbling and tremors quieted, and the dark clouds parted. Lucilius looked at the three crosses, his attention on the one in the middle.

"Why are we here?" he asked again.

"What does this place mean to you?"

"Nothing. Judgement was passed on the Nazarene. We executed the judgement. It is who we are, and it is what we do."

He dismissed the sound of wailing and lamenting coming from the women in the crowd. Their cries battered at his resolve to remain detached from what took place here two millennia ago.

"Did you ever wonder if the punishment was deserving?"

Gen's question took Lucilius's attention away from the tormenting cries. He shrugged. "That is for greater minds to decide. I was a soldier. I followed orders. There was simplicity in that."

"Then why have you refused to follow orders this time?"

Gen didn't know why she felt she had to ask these questions, but it felt right. She didn't fight the words that rose to her lips.

"Refused to follow orders? Speak plainly," Lucilius was irritated.

"Asmodeus gave you an order. Why did you decide to walk away?"

Lucilius grunted but didn't reply. He looked intently at Jesus Christ's cross. "He was weak," he murmured.

"Was He?" Gen countered, pointing at the cross. "He was humble—the epitome of humility—but He wasn't weak. He could have destroyed His enemies with a mere thought. Could have called legions of angels to His aid. But He chose not to. He had a goal, and He couldn't be deterred from it. What more of an example of strength could there be?"

Lucilius pondered on Gen's remarks, then turned away from the cross. "I tire of this drama," he said.

Gen could sense that their time in this moment was over.

"Come, let's see what else is in store for us." She grabbed hold of Lucilius's arm, and they blinked away.

Mark watched Gen and Lucilius carefully. There was great power at play here. He could feel it—more power than he had felt since he acquired the ability to sense the essence that flowed around everything and everyone.

Gen had her hand on Lucilius's arm. Her face was a picture of intense concentration, while Lucilius's was locked in a grimace of pain, frozen in anguish.

Myrddin looked just as uneasy as Mark. This was virgin territory. Neither of them knew what to do.

One wrong action on their part could harm Gen, so they watched and waited.

A baby's cry brought Gen back to the moment. She glanced around.

They were in a hut made of wood and clay, where a baby cried in a corner.

"What sorcery is this?"

Lucilius had backed into a corner. "Why are we here?" he snarled in anger.

"I don't know, but as I said earlier, we are only onlookers. We can't be hurt."

"Take me back immediately," he barked.

Gen was taken aback by Lucilius's rage. He pressed himself as much as he could against the wall with desperate eyes. He looked like a rabid dog.

"That's not how this works. We have to know and understand why we are here," Gen said gently.

"Take me back now. I don't want to be saved or delivered anymore. Take me back now."

Lucilius's voice rose to a scream, and he rushed at Gen.

Reacting on instinct, she raised her hands, and her power flared.

Lucilius screamed as the bright light washed over him, the pain pushing him backward. Gen immediately cut off the light and looked at Lucilius in worry. "What are you so afraid of?"

The baby's cry continued, and the hut's little wooden door opened, and a cold wind blew snowflakes inside. A boy of about ten years old walked in and struggled to shut the door quickly.

He walked to the baby and tried to soothe it, but it continued wailing, and the boy ended up crying as well.

"I do not have to see this," Lucilius whispered.

But there was no stopping the visions once they started. They needed to see it through.

"What's going on, Lucilius? Is that you? Is the little boy your brother?"

Gen felt her heart go out to both of them.

The baby's screaming continued. The little boy stood up and wiped his tears away.

Gen felt the air grow cold as he stood over the wailing baby.

No, Lucilius isn't the baby.

She recognized the same stance in the little boy as he braced himself on his feet. The same square of the shoulder and the way he tilted his head as though studying something of great importance.

The air continued to grow colder until Gen had to rub her hands together to try and get them warm.

Something happened here, in this little hut—something wrong, something unspeakable.

"What did you do?"

It came out as a whisper.

Suddenly, Gen didn't want to be there, either. She watched as little Lucilius picked up the crying baby and pushed open the hut's door with his shoulder.

He struggled against a gust of wind that threatened to bowl him off his feet. The baby cried louder as they stepped out into the harsh wind.

No!

Gen couldn't move. She stared in shock as the boy walked out of the warmth of the barren hut and into the freezing cold. The wailing grew faint as the little boy carried the baby away.

The wind slammed the door shut. Gen had no concept of how much time passed before it opened again.

The little boy returned to the hut—his face blue and streaked with frozen tear tracks—empty-handed. He walked to the corner where the baby had lain and slumped to the floor, hugged his knees to his chest, and rocked gently on the spot. In the opposite corner, Lucilius was on the floor in the exact same position.

"You didn't have to," Gen whispered. "It was a baby. There could have been another way."

Lucilius allowed Gen's sorrow to wash over him. A tiny tear ran down one of his cheeks.

"My father died in a senseless war. We were not Romans, nor citizens of Rome, so we were left to fend for ourselves. One day, our mother left. She said she was going to forage for food, but she never came back. I waited for three days. We were far from any settlement, and I was afraid of leaving my baby brother alone. By the fourth day, I knew she was never coming back. He wouldn't stop. I tried everything I remembered my mother doing; he just cried

192

and cried. On the fifth day, I knew I had to leave. I was too weak to think of carrying him along, not where I planned to go, anyway. His death seemed the only option."

Lucilius's words stunned Gen. She looked at him and only saw weary resignation.

"So, tell me, Nail Bearer, can your Nazarene really redeem me?" he spat. "My little brother was just the first in an endless line. The next to die was my dear mother. I tracked her down in a nearby town, playing the harlot with a local. A knife across the throat was too good an ending for her. I was cursed even before I was damned to wander the face of the earth. Can your Nazarene cleanse these hands from the countless innocent blood they have been dipped in? Tell me, Nail Bearer, can He?"

Gen was silent. Lucilius had finally left his corner, and he now loomed over Gen, pure rage in his eyes.

The cold in the room bit into her soul. She didn't know what to say.

Had Mark been right all along? Were some people irredeemable? Was Lucilius marked for death and destruction?

She refused to believe that.

He who the Son sets free is free indeed.

The words were like a balm to her aching soul. Didn't the Bible say that all had sinned, and that we were all destined for destruction, if not for Calvary?

"Your crimes can never be too black that His blood can't wash them clean. The choice is yours.

Do you want to be saved? I don't stand in judgement of you, Lucilius, and, you know what? Neither should you."

As Gen spoke, she saw Lucilius as God did. He was a different person, one who walked in God's forgiveness. It was possible—a branch in destiny that could snap into reality. Gen saw light around Lucilius in an instant in time. Truly, Lucilius could be saved if he chose to be.

That was when the darkness struck.

13

Thick black fog moved in a serpentine motion as the mist solidified before Gen's eyes. The acrid smell of sulphur filled her nostrils and stung her eyes. She broke into a bout of coughing as she looked for a way out.

The serpentine fog gathered into a humanoid shape, and Gen saw two reptilian eyes focus on Lucilius and herself.

"My, what do we have here? Lucilius, Lucilius. What a naughty boy you've been."

The words hissed out of the figure's mouth with a click of its tongue. Gen leaped as far away as she could from the black fog surrounding it. The humanoid shape looked like a twisted genie from an evil lamp; it wavered in and out of her sight, leaving ghostly apparitions in the air.

Gen knew what it was.

"I'm not afraid of you, Serpent," she said bravely.

The figure chuckled in amusement.

"That is of little consequence, Nail Bearer. This is my domain, and my mark is on this one."

The figure coiled like a snake and moved its head to survey the room.

"Ah, such sweet memories. The younger they are, the greater their propensity to imagine violence and destruction. This one had it from an early age. My mark was imprinted on him from the very night he slew his brother."

"But he desires to be free from you," Gen proclaimed.

"His desires are futile. He is mine. He will always be mine. Now and forevermore." The figure chuckled again, filling the tiny space with its rumble.

Gen saw that Lucilius seemed resigned to his fate. He stood in a docile manner, shoulders slumped, staring at the shape in the fog with weary acceptance.

"He lies, Lucilius. He is the father of lies. You can be free. Your life can begin afresh."

"Enough of this," the figure hissed.

"Leave here while you can, Nail Bearer. This one can never be yours. My hold on him is infinite."

Gen grabbed Lucilius by the shoulders and shook him. "Is this the great Lucilius? Conqueror of nations? Are you so blind that you cannot see the truth? The serpent can't have you without your acceptance of his dominion. Resist him, Lucilius. Fight him by accepting the truth."

The figure hissed again and flew across the room. It struck at Gen, opening its mouth to expose sharp fangs. She reacted quickly, bright light flared around her, and the figure slammed into it, trying to crush her with its vast power.

"Choose, Lucilius. Choose now who you will obey. This is your opportunity for change."

The humanoid shape laughed again and slammed into her white shield.

Gen's arms trembled from holding the light burning around her.

The figure was toying with her, allowing her to drain her essence until she was unprotected before it.

She felt anger rise in her throat, and she held onto it. She was a child of the light, and she would never bow to the darkness. The light around her flared brighter, burning hotter than she had ever seen.

The figure paused in mid-flight and studied Gen.

"You are strong, little one, but the end is inevitable. I have access to your world through this being you wish to give your life attempting to save him. I will make a trade with you, Nail Bearer. You may keep this being, but in exchange, you will choose which one I will rip apart in torment. The wizard or the protector."

"No!" Gen growled. "You cannot have them. You cannot leave here."

"That is where you are wrong, little flower. This cursed one is a portal to the material plane. I only need a moment to execute my wrath. I will lay waste to your abode and the quaint little town you call home."

The figure continued laughing as an image of its humanoid form slammed into Lucilius.

Fear clenched Gen's muscles. The figure still stood before her, but Gen knew that her loved ones were in danger.

Mark felt the essence around Gen and Lucilius churn and stepped back.

"Something's wrong, Myrddin," he said in alarm.

He didn't know what it was, but he was certain something powerful was happening. Black steam rose from Lucilius's body and began to take shape, condensing to form the outline of a man.

The being suspended in the air and looked down on Mark and Myrddin, then laughed and spewed out fire.

Myrddin jumped in front of Mark and conjured a tornado of air. The creature's fire slammed into it, and fire spun in a huge circle in front of them.

"What is going on?" Mark shouted over the roaring tornado of flames.

"I don't know, but I can't hold this much longer."

Mark looked uncertainly at Gen and Lucilius. The entity came from Lucilius's body. Would taking Lucilius out would stop the laughing creature?

He paused.

Would killing Lucilius harm Gen? Was he willing to take that risk?

Mark knew he would have to make a decision soon.

Lucilius was lost.

Recalling the moment he had left his baby brother out in the cold drained his last ounce of willpower.

He had loved his brother. As a kid, he enjoyed hearing his cooing and watching him grow. His laughter dampened the harsh reality of the cruel world he was born into.

He saw Gen battle his master and could only pity her.

He was a lost cause, and his demise would benefit the world.

But her foolish words wouldn't leave his mind.

You can be set free.

They burrowed deep into his soul, latching on to a part he thought had died in that little hut eons ago.

You can be set free.

Did he deserve it? Definitely not.

Did he want it?

Lucilius felt a stirring in the depths of his soul—a longing for something better, the warmth he felt as a little boy when he looked at his baby brother.

The desire spread, and he felt a tiny flicker of light spark within him. He held onto the flicker and fed it the little boy's hopes and dreams for a better life.

Yes, he wanted to be free.

And Lucilius screamed it out loud.

The figure screamed in anger and frustration at Lucilius's rejection of its hold over him.

"You fool," it snarled. "You could have ruled by my side, laid waste to the pitiful existence of the life here. You threw that all away for HIM?" The last word was shouted as the figure summoned the vastness of its power.

Bright light enveloped Gen and Lucilius, and she saw the image of the hut dissolve.

They were standing in an open field, with rich wheat stalks all around them. She looked around and was relieved to see the serpent was gone.

Lucilius was on his knees some feet away, shining with a bright light.

"You are free," Gen said.

Lucilius looked at himself in amazement. "It's like...being blind and then having your sight back. Everything looks...different."

"I know what you're talking about. But you know what this means, don't you?"

Lucilius looked up from staring at his hands.

"It's gone. It's all gone," he said softly.

"Yes. The darkness has fled from your soul but has also taken that which it gave. You're human once again. Can you live with that?"

"It was a two-sided coin, Nail Bearer. The power ate at the soul and took away as much as it gave. It's like a great weight has been lifted off my shoulders. And why do I want to smile all of a sudden?"

"It's called joy, Lucilius. It's contagious, and it feeds the soul, making you a better you."

Gen smiled at the curious expression on Lucilius's face. She had always had her granddad guiding her and showing her the right path to take in life. Lucilius looked like a toddler realizing that it could take little steps without falling.

"Where are we, Nail Bearer?"

The vast field looked familiar, but Gen couldn't place where she had seen it before. The air shimmered, and Lucilius stepped back defensively as Baraqiel appeared.

Gen realized she could make out the angel's features. He was handsome, in an aristocratic sort of way. An inner light shone from his eyes, and his golden hair fell to his shoulders. He wore chainmail and a breastplate over his clothes, and when he looked at her, Gen could have sworn she saw a smile, or the semblance of one, on the angel's face.

"Light Bringer," Baraqiel addressed Gen. "You have done well."

She still found the angel's voice hard to contain as her soul vibrated in resonance. She saw Lucilius stagger and fall to one knee.

"You know, I'm beginning to agree with Mark that you pick the worst times to appear."

"I would have come earlier, but the evil one's forces detained me."

"So, why are you here?"

"To guide you back. The accuser isn't happy to have lost this one. My presence will ensure you arrive back in your time safely."

Baraqiel pointed to the shimmering portal he had come through.

One moment, Mark thought the shield would fail, and the next, the entity disappeared. Myrddin sucked in a deep breath and tried to regain his essence. Mark hurried to Gen's side to see her turn to him and smile.

"Did you miss me?" she teased.

He laughed and pulled her into a hug. Lucilius stirred and raised his head.

"You did it," Mark gasped. He could see Lucilius was different. The black essence Mark associated with the accursed was gone, and his whole presence had changed.

Myrddin walked over and patted Gen's shoulder. He could see the exhaustion on her face underneath all the excitement.

"I don't expect it wasn't easy," he said.

"You can only imagine, Granddad."

He nodded and flicked his hand. The bands of air holding Lucilius down evaporated, and he rubbed his wrists as he was released.

"What do we do with him?" Myrddin asked.

"He's a free man, Granddad. He can do whatever he wants to do."

"I'd advise keeping him here for a few days," Mark said. He saw Gen frown at him and quickly added, "For his safety, of course."

"I agree with the Protector," Lucilius grunted. "It would be wiser to keep me here for a while."

"You are not a prisoner, Lucilius," Gen said, shaking her head.

"Then you are not as wise as I'd thought, Nail Bearer. Wizard, don't you agree with the summation of the nail bearer's protector?"

Gen grunted inwardly. Lucilius may be redeemed, but he maintained his archaic way of talking, and it was giving her a headache. "You can call us by our names, Lucilius. The same way we call you by yours."

"He does have a point," Myrddin said. "He needs to stay. No, he's not a prisoner. You may have converted him, but it wouldn't be wise to leave him exposed to his former lifestyle. Asmodeus could revert all the work you put in getting him to this point."

Gen saw that her granddad did have a point. And, yes, Mark was right, too. But he hadn't said it the way her granddad had. Mark saw the look she gave him and raised an eyebrow.

"You need to take some communication classes from Granddad."

"Why? Do I need to learn another language?"

"No, but..."

Gen saw the smile on Mark's face and punched his shoulder.

Lucilius looked between the two of them and couldn't decide if he wanted their camaraderie or to throw up in disgust.

The air shimmered. Baraqiel appeared.

"Myrddin, you are needed once more to forge a weapon to fight the tide of darkness. Gather the nails and bring out the anvil. We must prepare for war."

Myrddin dragged out his anvil, hammer, and work tools. He had promised himself ages ago that he would never make an enchanted weapon of legendary level, but the dire present circumstance called for it.

If Baraqiel was to be believed—and he was an angel, after all—Myrddin's expertise would be called forth again.

Making a sword was straightforward: get the steel, shape it, forge it, voilà, a weapon was ready. Making a legendary sword might entail the same steps, but it was astronomically more difficult.

Reforging a broken sword was a totally different ballgame, and this last option was what Myrddin had in mind. They didn't have the time for him to invest spells, sigils, and runes on the ingot to be used, but he had a shortcut.

He placed the broken pieces of Mark's sword on the anvil and arranged them.

The sword was bonded to Mark on an elemental level; his blood and essence had bled into it. Building the broken sword back to its original strength would usually have proven nearly impossible, but Myrddin had two factors in his favour: he had three nails and an angel.

He ignored everyone around him and began a silent chant to focus his essence while he placed the nails on the broken pieces.

The plan was to leapfrog the whole forging—or, in this case, reforging—process by providing fire of greater power and heat. The nails would act as glue to hold the old pieces together, and the flames would work the metal back to its original form.

Baraqiel walked over and looked at the broken sword on the anvil.

"This is a wise choice," his voice vibrated.

"We will have to do this together," Myrddin replied.

Baraqiel moved to the opposite side of the anvil and placed his hands over it. Myrddin mirrored the angel's stance and nodded.

Essence radiated from Baraqiel, and Myrddin felt more power than he had ever experienced flow into the sword pieces. He added his spell, speaking words of power that shook the air around the barn.

Mark couldn't take his eyes away from the process occurring before him. He felt as if his bones would shatter into a thousand tiny pieces as Baraqiel's life-force slammed into the sword. The sword morphed before Mark's eyes. The nails dissolved and seeped into the molten sword, binding the pieces together. The sword began to glow brighter, and Mark had to squint his eyes from the brightness. The very air shook and vibrated with energy. He dimly made out some of the words Myrddin chanted.

"...daemonium interfectorem...olethros... horsek...harbinger to evil and darkness's destruction...demon slayer...balm giver..."

Each phrase released power and rattled the anvil as it sank into the sword. When the last word was spoken, the air around the anvil exploded, throwing Mark, Lucilius, and Gen backward. Myrddin's body blazed with more power than the naked eye could see. He rose above the ground as his body became a conduit that channelled the essence of his will into the sword.

Baraqiel cut off his powers, and Myrddin slowly floated back to the ground. The brightness around the anvil reduced, and Mark saw the sword whole. It shone with the brightness of the sun and pulsated with power.

Myrddin beckoned Mark over, and he slowly obeyed. The air around the anvil remained thick with magic, and he had to use his hands to push through an invisible barrier it created.

"Pick up the sword," Myrddin's voice radiated with energy, sending shockwaves around the barn. Mark gritted his teeth when the waves reached him; it felt similar to when Baraqiel spoke.

Mark picked up the sword and was stunned at how light it felt in his hand. He could feel the power residing within it, and his whole arm tingled from the vibration it seemed to hum.

"Cut this."

Myrddin tossed something at Mark, and he responded instantly. He swung the sword. A millisecond later, two halves of a copper coin landed on the ground.

"Now, cut my arm."

Myrddin stretched out his right arm. Mark hesitated, and he could sense Gen shuffling uneasily, but he saw the serious look in Myrddin's eyes and nodded. He raised the sword.

Mark almost lost his footing as the sword passed through Myrddin's arm. He gasped in amazement. Myrddin created a sword of compressed air and lunged at Mark.

He parried the attack and was surprised to see sparks as their swords clashed. Myrddin lunged again, and he swung to parry again, but at the last moment, Myrddin released his sword of air. Mark stared in shock as his sword passed through the wizard's chest, leaving him unharmed.

"I'm sure you must have figured it out by now," Myrddin said with a smile.

Mark nodded. He was too emotional for words.

He couldn't accidentally hurt anyone with the sword. It was the perfect weapon: able to defend him and yet not be a risk to others.

"The sword cannot cut animate bodies," Lucilius reasoned.

"But how can it tell the difference?" Gen had felt her heart jump into her throat when Mark swung at her granddad. She had expected something to happen but had been unprepared for what she had seen. "Can I hold it?" she asked.

Mark passed her the sword. It was light, and the presence of the nails within it made it feel like one big nail to her.

"May I?" Lucilius asked, and Gen looked at Mark for confirmation. He frowned at the request but nodded all the same.

Gen was glad. She knew the risk they were taking in trusting Lucilius with a weapon, and she appreciated that Mark was willing to extend an olive branch. That, and the fact that they knew the sword couldn't harm any of them.

She gave the sword to Lucilius, and the moment it touched his hand, he grunted, and the sword hit the ground.

"What trickery is this? The sword is heavier than a boulder used as a temple foundation."

Mark picked up the sword and twirled it. He handed it back to Gen, who tried to spin it like Mark did, causing him to smile at her effort.

Lucilius stretched out his hand for it again, and Gen gave it to him. This time, he held on, but he could barely raise the tip.

"What of you, Wizard?" Lucilius grunted as he handed it back to Gen. She gave the sword to her granddad, and he held it, though the strain of keeping it up was visible on Myrddin's face.

"The sword is Mark's. Any other person must bear the burden and the sacrifices that his lineage carries. Being a protector cannot be taken lightly."

"But I could carry it easily," Gen pointed out.

"Because you are the nail bearer," Mark responded. That was the only answer that made sense to him. Knowing that no other person could hold onto it was an added boon for him.

"You're partly right, Mark. Add that to her new abilities—the sword must sense the light in her."

"Asmodeus gathers his forces for a final push. You have a day or two before the confrontation," Baraqiel interrupted. The angel looked at Gen. "Gather your people."

The air shimmered, and he was gone.

"You know, he could have stuck around for the fight," Mark said and shook his head.

"He protects us from fights we're not even aware of," Gen said.

Gen was grateful for the help Baraqiel brought. Now all she had to do was find a way to protect everyone.

14

CONSTANTINOPLE, 327 A.D.

Queen Helena wasn't happy that the accursed had escaped, but she was glad the raid was a success. The emperor's guards had rounded up all the people who were at the amphitheatre. It took a while, but they had sorted through the crowd. Separating the ignorant had been the right path to take. The ring leaders weren't spared, though, and Helena was sorry for the lives that had to be taken due to the accurseds' plan to overthrow the emperor.

As much as she would have liked to spare the men, the emperor was explicit in his orders. Anyone found guilty of inciting or sponsoring members to incite the crowd to create havoc couldn't be forgiven; the punishment was death.

Three members of the senate were captured during the raid and, after interrogation, had given names of other members who had been involved.

So, Helena wasn't surprised to see Dux Aurelius sitting in front of her in her living quarters. She waited for him to speak, though she had an idea of what the senator wanted from her.

"I love the emperor and would never think of subverting his leadership or rule. This must be the work of Cassius," Aurelius lamented.

He accused the spymaster Cassius in every other sentence that came out of his mouth and, truthfully, it was getting tiring.

Helena sensed Calisto adjust his stance as he stood behind her. Aurelius had ordered Calisto out of the room, but he had ignored the Dux, simply feigning ignorance. That, or Calisto hoped the Dux would try to remove him from the room physically. Helena had a suspicion that it was the latter.

After hearing Aurelius refer to the spymaster numerous times, she almost wished Calisto would evict the loud-mouthed coward from her parlor.

She smiled gently as she stilled her thoughts.

The men in the senate could try the patience of a saint.

"Dux Aurelius, as much as I sympathize with your present predicament, you must know I don't have any influence in matters of politics."

Helena wasn't lying. She was the dowager, the mother of the powerful Emperor Constantine the Great. But there was a limit to how she could bend the emperor to her will. She had little say when it regarded political matters. Had the Dux come regarding issues that bordered on the spiritual or religious, he would have stood a better chance of getting the answer he wanted from her.

Not that she would lose any sleep over any judgment made against Dux Aurelius. The man was a snake, and there was irrefutable evidence he had knowingly sponsored dissidents with the intention of causing instability in the city.

His future was out of her hands.

"My empress, there must be something you can do. This is all lies, I tell you, lies spread by my archenemy Cassius. It is all his doing. He eyes my position, empress. He wishes to see me fall from grace."

Helena pinched the bridge of her nose to relieve the throbbing headache that began the moment he knocked on her doors.

She knew what her son planned for the traitors in the senate.

There would be a series of *accidents*. The emperor didn't want the citizenry to lose heart in the leadership of the ruling council. Their crimes would never see the light of day, but justice would be served.

She had only been able to plead for the families of the traitors. Her son planned to weed out every seed of rebellion, even if it had meant persecuting the innocent, who were only guilty by association or kinship.

She couldn't have stood idly by and let that happen. Helena was glad she had been able to convince her son to be lenient.

The guilty would be punished, but only the guilty.

Calisto had supported the emperor's brand of justice, but Helena had stayed her ground.

Dux Aurelius had been officially relieved of his position and duties on the grounds of ill health.

He was here to beg for clemency, unaware that his banishment to his villa would be his final resting place.

Aurelius would not be coming back to Constantinople.

"I will see what I can do, Dux Aurelius. I will talk to the emperor, but I cannot guarantee success in this endeavour."

He brightened up and showered Helena with accolades. She felt bad, but she did plan on pleading to her son on behalf of all the traitors.

She just knew that his stance wouldn't change.

The Dux got to his feet and left her living quarters, and Helena relaxed in her seat. She smoothed her blue gown over her legs. That was her last meeting for the day.

"I am getting too old for this, Calisto."

Queen Helena didn't get any response from Calisto, so she turned to address him.

"What do you have to say, Calisto?"

Calisto remained on guard at her back. He grunted in reply, but Helena waited for him to voice his opinion. She may not always agree with his pattern of dispersing justice, but she knew his heart was always in the right place, and his wisdom was great for such a young man.

"I can see your desire to express your opinion written all over your face, young man. Speak your mind before you explode."

"You are too easy on them, My Queen. An example needs to be made of the traitors. This would ensure that any others with thoughts of rebellion would think twice."

"But it will not stop the rebellious."

"Steel and bloodshed will quell any rebellious inclination."

Helena harrumphed in irritation. "I know in that thick skull of yours resides more than the thoughts of a killer."

Her words brought an uncomfortable silence, and she almost wished she could take them back, but sometimes Calisto needed to stop acting as a Praetorian guard.

"I didn't mean any offence, Calisto."

"I'm aware of that, My Queen. I was just surprised that you saw more than any other."

"Because I have seen your heart. You desire to protect. And though you were brought up in the arena, you don't always think that way. You are a good man, Calisto."

His response was cut off by a knock, and the door opened. Merlin walked in and flopped into the seat Aurelius had vacated minutes ago.

"The bleeding accursed are nowhere to be found," Merlin said wearily.

"So, we can say we have won? Driven them out of the city?" Helena said, wishing out loud.

Calisto grunted again, and Helena sighed. "You know this strong, silent male approach grates on my nerves. What's on your mind, Calisto?"

"I don't think now would be a good time to relax our guard. We shouldn't assume they are gone. They aren't powerless," Calisto stated.

"Why do you think so?" she asked.

"This would be the ideal time to strike. If we assume they are defeated and have run away with their tails between their legs, we will become lax and complacent. A well-planned assault will catch us with our...eh...will catch us unaware."

Helena looked to Merlin for his take on Calisto's assessment.

"He's right. I won't be surprised if they decide to strike back at us," Merlin said.

"And when do you project this attack will come?" Helena asked Merlin.

"Tonight," Calisto answered for Merlin.

Calisto felt Merlin's gaze on him as Queen Helena turned around.

"Tonight? But won't our guard be up?" she asked.

"Yes."

"But you just said they'd wait for a time when we had relaxed our guard."

"And tonight would be ideal. We would think that an attack so soon would be impossible, and without consciously acting that way, our guard would be lax."

Helena turned to Merlin again with a look of apprehension.

"I must confess, Calisto seems to be making a great deal of sense," Merlin shrugged.

"So, what do we do then?" Queen Helena asked in worry.

Calisto gripped the pommel of his sword. "We set a trap of our own," he smiled.

Helena tried to feign sleeping but couldn't succeed at stilling her beating heart.

The night was silent, save for the occasional cries of nocturnal animals that roamed the city looking for prey.

Tonight would decide if she was prey or predator.

She knew Calisto and Merlin were nearby, but for the plan to work, they refrained from letting her know exactly where they would be positioned. They also advised maintaining the same security detail and structure so the accursed didn't get wind of their plans.

It was all right for them to plan, but she was the bait. She was the one who had to wait and hope they were both wrong, that the enemy had indeed fled.

As the night wore on, Helena began to feel an unease that had nothing to do with her precarious position.

Her spirit was troubled.

Something was going down tonight.

The night masked a shadow that scaled the palace wall with ease. The figure landed quietly and seemed to disappear as it blended with the dark shadows that filled the corners of the palace walls.

A guard marching past didn't see the figure rise. He didn't feel the short sword that plunged into his heart as he was dragged into nearby shadows.

Death had come stalking the palace of Constantinople.

Calisto listened and waited.

From his hiding place, he had a clear view of the door leading to Queen Helena's quarters. She queen had been reluctant to agree to the plan, and not just for her own safety.

People could die to guarantee the plan's success, and Queen Helena hadn't been able to accept that.

Calisto finally agreed to alert the palace guards of the possibility of an attack tonight, which had placated her. He hadn't told her that alerting the guards wasn't an assurance the accursed wouldn't claim unsuspecting lives. If he had, she would have called off the ambush.

Calisto and the guards understood what it meant to lay their lives down for their queen. They would sacrifice themselves if it meant protecting her or guaranteeing her safety.

Calisto heard a scuffle at the end of the walkway leading to the queen's quarters.

They had taken the bait—the accursed were here.

Calisto couldn't see them, but he was convinced he was right. Having fought them repeatedly, he could somehow sense when they were at play.

A guard went to check the disturbance, and Calisto heard the thud of a sharp object piercing through flesh. A moment later, the gurgle of a dying man reached his ears.

Calisto's heart went out to the guard, but he restrained himself from bursting out of his hiding place. Their sacrifices wouldn't be in vain if they eradicated the accursed tonight.

He heard the twang of a bow, and an arrow whistled through the air. One of the guards by the door to the queen's quarters clutched his chest and collapsed. The second reacted swiftly, his sword smacking the second arrow away from piercing him.

Calisto gritted his teeth. These were his men dying out there.

A clash of swords and the second guard fell with a slice to the throat.

Calisto saw more than one figure rush into the queen's quarters.

It was time to spring the trap.

Queen Helena heard the door to her bed chambers burst open and knew that death had come for her.

She had fooled herself in hoping the accursed wouldn't come, that blood wouldn't be shed this night.

They wouldn't stop. These accursed would spread death and destruction wherever they went.

Helena knew she wouldn't shed a tear if the lives of the accursed were snuffed out. Maybe that would compensate for all the innocent lives they had taken.

Four figures rushed in. One of the assailants rushed to the bed and plunged his sword into the body lying in it.

Immediately, bright light flooded the room, and the four turned and shielded their eyes.

Calisto and Merlin rushed in.

Merlin blasted a gust of wind at the assassins. His spell washed over a force field around the figures, but he didn't hesitate. The air above the four charged and sparked with lightning, and Merlin's hand swept down.

The assassins screamed as a thousand jolts of electricity surged through them. Merlin continued the onslaught even as the assassin's clothes burst into flames.

An arrow flew from their midst, and Calisto moved quickly to bat it aside. He and Merlin were coordinated and well-prepared.

They would strike quickly and lethally with magic, and Calisto would act as a guard to protect Merlin from any mundane attack.

The assassin on the bed quickly recovered and rolled off, dodging Merlin's lightning strike and charging.

Merlin flung a gust of wind, but he sliced through it with his sword.

Calisto moved to intercept him. Their swords clashed while Merlin concentrated on his next spell.

Calisto knew who this charging assassin was. He deflected a slice to his neck and spun with a counter. He had fought Lucilius too many times not to know his style of attack. Their swords clashed repeatedly, and Calisto grunted as he felt Lucilius's sword slice his arm, drawing blood. He ignored the wound. It was shallow and hadn't nicked any vein or artery. He ducked under another swing, stabbing forward. Lucilius stepped back, and Merlin blasted him with another gust of wind. The force of the wind knocked Lucilius off his already unbalanced feet, and he rolled away to avoid Calisto's downward swing.

Merlin saw Atticus fling fire in his direction, and he slapped it away with contempt.

They may be immortals, but their prowess in the magical arts was pitiful. He heard the twang of an arrow leaving its bow and created a shield to deflect it.

This was stage one of Merlin and Calisto's plan. They had successfully contained the accursed.

It was now time for stage two.

Marius was the weak link of the group. While his word of power was strong, Merlin and Calisto were immune, and he was useless in a fight without it. Remus would attack from a distance, as was his wont.

Merlin wove spells quickly in the air and cast a time-limiting effect around the room. The accursed slowed down.

A band on Calisto's arm flashed brightly; he moved at normal speed. Merlin had enchanted the armband to make him resilient to the time-limiting spell. Calisto batted away Lucilius's sluggish attempt to cut him and replied with a thrust that buried his sword deep into his stomach.

Lucilius grunted in pain and clutched the sword. Calisto let go of the other end and brought out a curved dagger.

They would end the accursed tonight.

Merlin grunted as he bore the weight of holding the time-limiting spell. He couldn't move, or the spell would shatter.

Atticus moved in slow motion, trying to weave a fireball, but the door burst open before he could complete it. More guards hurried in, all wearing armbands.

Atticus's eyes widened in alarm and fear as one of the guards rushed at him. His fireball fizzled into nothing as the sword plunged into his stomach.

Within moments, the accursed were surrounded, and Merlin believed the trap could rid him of them once and for all.

Calisto struck with the dagger, but Lucilius moved at the last moment, and it embedded in his shoulder instead of his throat. He rode the blow and spun, unsheathing a hidden dagger. Calisto watched it leave Lucilius's hand and move at normal speed.

No one could stop the dagger's flight toward Merlin's chest.

The wizard staggered back as it punched into his body. Pain blossomed; his spell shattered. The disruption of his magic created a backlash that slammed into him and threw him across the room.

Calisto pulled out his last dagger and rushed for Marius. Now back to their normal, supernatural speed, Atticus immediately created a portal that he and Remus ran through. Calisto slammed into Marius, who was trying to reach the portal. He stabbed him in the chest and then punched his sword's pommel to drive the blade as deep as possible.

Marius fell, screaming in pain. Guards swarmed him, stabbing him repeatedly. Calisto looked away in time to see Lucilius stagger through the portal, which snapped shut behind him.

Merlin grunted as he pulled out the dagger from his chest. The pain was excruciating but not life-threatening.

"Why aren't you healing yourself?" Calisto asked, running to his side.

"Doesn't work that way. It's the price to pay to have a healing spell. I can't cast it on myself. But don't worry, I'll live."

Calisto grunted and smiled. "We have one of them. We caught Marius."

The corner of Merlin's mouth lifted in a twisted grin. "Good."

15

Lucilius walked into the sitting room, where he was met with gasps and looks of terror. "Why is he here?" Isabella asked the unspoken question.

"He's here because he's one of us now," Gen answered.

"He can't be one of us," Josephine said.

"Well, he's not one of them. I can guarantee you that. Lucilius was once an enemy, but now...he is... not that anymore," Gen said.

Could Lucilius be called a friend? she wondered.

Gen couldn't blame the others for not welcoming Lucilius with open arms, but she had seen a glimpse of his past. The good she saw there was the lynchpin that had set him free.

"He will be here with us for a little while. I know some here have history with Lucilius, none more than my granddad, and he is willing to accept him.

I think in light of that, it would be unkind to do otherwise."

"He tried to kill me," Josephine said.

"Me too," Isabella added.

Lucilius grunted and was about to speak, then thought it wise to remain silent. He sensed that what happened at that moment could shape his future.

"Like I said, we all have history with him. Let's give him a chance. That's all I'm asking for."

"And as impossible as it may seem, Lucilius is a changed man." Mark stepped forward and looked at the people in the room.

He may have his reservations, but if he was honest with himself, his opinions were biased against Lucilius. But he had seen what he had seen. "We have bigger problems presently. We need to plan for Asmodeus."

"Is that a sword in your hand?" O'Neal asked.

Mark sighed.

"Yes, it is a sword."

"Wow, that's fantastic. I've always had a fascination for swords. Even joined Swordmakers Online." O'Neal walked to Mark and admired it.

"Can I hold it?"

"I don't think that would be—"

"Just to get the feel. Never held a real sword in my hands before."

"I'm not sure you'll be able to hold it," Mark said with a frown. He saw the disappointment on O'Neal's face and changed his mind.

"The sword is unique. It can—"

"I know I just joined the group, and we don't know each other. If you really don't want me touching your sword, all you have to do is say so."

Mark looked to Gen and Myrddin for help, but Gen only shrugged.

Reluctantly, Mark handed the sword to O'Neal, extending the hilt of the sword first.

O'Neal's face beamed as he accepted the sword, grasping the pommel with both hands.

Immediately, it dragged his hands down, and the tip struck the floor.

"What the bloody hell?" O'Neal exclaimed.

The rest of the group gathered around him in surprise.

"It's an enchanted sword," Isabella said in excitement.

"There's no such thing as an enchanted sword," O'Neal grunted, trying to lift it again.

"Never heard of Excalibur?" Isabella asked.

"Excalibur isn't real. It is a fairy tale for children."

"I would have agreed with you some days back, but with what I've seen, I'd be a fool is deny it," Josephine joined in.

"It's a trick. Maybe it's a loaded sword. Or Mark may have a magnet on his person."

"I think it's real," Theo said. He was beginning to understand what Gen meant when she'd said he wouldn't believe her. How could she have explained any of this? He had heard screams from the barn, but Lucilius didn't look hurt. Theo he wished he could have been there. He didn't know what happened

227

in the barn, but the man who walked out looked different. Lucilius seemed relaxed—almost carefree.

O'Neal looked in amazement as Mark took the sword back, and the ease with which he held it.

"I don't know what Asmodeus has planned, but we believe he'll most likely strike tonight. Again, we would like you all to remain in this sitting room throughout the night. You'll be safe here," Mark said.

"I want to help," Josephine said. She saw the look of uncertainty in Mark's eyes and quickly added, "And I can help. Just ask the police dude over there."

Gen saw Theo nod. She hadn't heard there was anything special about Josephine, but she had expected as much. That had been the purpose of taking her along for the visions. "What are you saying, Josephine?"

"I don't know how to explain it, but last night, during the...fight, I came out to help, and it seems I can...I don't know, run very fast?"

"I don't get it," Gen said.

"We realized the creatures couldn't cross through the front door for some reason, so Josephine decided to bait them through," Theo explained. "But one of them got a hold of her before she could get back inside from the porch, and when it was about to strike...I don't know. I didn't really see anything after that, but the next moment, the creature and Josephine came through the door together."

"I just knew that things wouldn't be good for me if it struck me, so I think I ran...very fast."

"Time displacement," Myrddin said, a thoughtful expression on his face.

"What?" she asked.

"You slowed time. It's a very rare gift, Miss Josephine. The ability to compress time. It made it seem like you ran very fast, but what you actually did was slow every other person down."

"You're kidding me," Isabella said.

"This is beginning to sound like…" Josephine started.

"What of me? What can I do?" O'Neal asked.

"So, you believe now?" Isabella taunted, and Gen smiled.

"I can't really say, Doctor, but we can find out if you're willing." She offered him her hand.

"Is this going to hurt or anything like that?" he asked suspiciously.

Gen shook her head. O'Neal looked at Gen, then at her outstretched hand. Finally, he sighed and put his in hers.

The world shifted.

Gen was glad O'Neal didn't scream or freak out when they reappeared elsewhere.

He looked around and took a deep breath. "Even the air smells different," he said after a while. "How are you doing it?"

"You still doubt, Doctor?"

"Not exactly, just curious, I guess. Unless I'm hallucinating or…"

"Look around, Doctor. Can you figure out where we are?"

Three crucifixion crosses loomed above them on a hill. People stood all around, some weeping, others taunting the dying men.

O'Neal hadn't grown up hearing many Bible stories, but he knew what he was seeing. He could just make out the man hanging on the left speak.

"You claim to be the Christ. Do something, then. Save yourself—and me."

"Quiet!" the other man on the right whispered harshly through his agony. "Don't you fear God? We were rightfully condemned for our actions, but this man before us is innocent." He tried to turn his face toward the man being crucified on the middle cross. "Remember me when you come into your kingdom, Lord."

"Truly, you will be with me in paradise today," Jesus said.

O'Neal turned to Gen. "Why am I seeing this?"

"I don't know. I don't control the visions. It's unique for each of us. But it's also related to what we need to see to believe."

Time passed, and Jesus cried out in a loud voice.

O'Neal saw the clouds shift and darken, and he heard the earth rumble. "Even if this is real, the question is *why*. Why did he have to suffer?" He couldn't quite place it. The crucifixion went contrary to other forms of religious beliefs. Why would a saviour have to suffer? He didn't understand.

Then, it hit him.

"It's what he said to the thief. Or rather what they said to each other." O'Neal turned to Gen with an excited look. "One of the thieves understood the meaning of the crucifixion. It's substitution. Someone had to pay the price for our reckless behaviour. The other thief didn't get that. He didn't want to accept his fault. He wanted Jesus to free him without acknowledging that he had erred."

O'Neal saw it now, and with that knowledge, he felt a deeper sense opening within him. The truth of things.

"I think I get it now. What I'm supposed to do."

Gen smiled and grasped O'Neal's arm.

The world went white.

O'Neal staggered back and looked at Gen in amazement. He saw her in a swirl of light. He noticed Mark's sword lit the whole room and wondered why he hadn't seen it before.

Before, I was blind.

"This is…" He didn't have a word to describe what he was seeing. He looked at the sword again and noticed the pattern on it. "It's beautiful. There seem to be different types of light radiating from it. Like different…I don't know…surges? I can't think of a better word. One layered over the other."

Myrddin's eyebrow shot up as they all looked at O'Neal in surprise.

"Baraqiel had a hand in the sword's reforging," Myrddin said.

"Baraqiel is the angel? Then that would be the brightest light I'm seeing. It's blazing. Like a sun approaching supernova. There's also another light with a silver hue that looks a lot like her," O'Neal nodded in Gen's direction.

It was blinding but didn't hurt his eyes. The final type of light he saw had a bluish overtone. "The last light looks a lot like your granddad's."

"That is...amazing." Gen was happy for O'Neal.

"I can't see anything. The sword looks normal to me," Isabella said.

O'Neal realized he was getting light-headed and tried to steady himself. He felt a hand grip him gently and guide him to a seat.

"That happened to me, too," Josephine said.

As he passed out on the sofa, O'Neal wondered what the rest of the world would look like now.

Mark sat on the porch with his sword laid across his lap and watched the sun go down. He heard footsteps approaching but didn't bother to turn.

"What is your plan for when Asmodeus comes?" Lucilius leaned on the banister on the porch, facing the setting sun.

Mark thought of ignoring the question, then changed his mind. If they were to accept Lucilius into the fold, they had to do it wholeheartedly, no matter how painful it was.

"Repel him. Like before."

"It won't be the same as before. He will have some surprises this time."

"And we have some of our own."

There was an uncomfortable moment of silence as Mark and Lucilius each fidgeted, trying to be polite.

"I know you don't like me, and you don't trust me. I do not blame you. I know I would do worse in your position."

"You're right. I don't like you, and I definitely don't trust you…but…one thing I've come to realize is that trust can be earned," Mark said gravely, staring into Lucilius's eyes. "I have one goal, to keep Gen safe, and I will go to great lengths to ensure that."

Lucilius nodded and looked around the ranch. "Do you feel it? This place?"

"Feel what?" Mark said.

"The power in this place."

"That would be Myrddin's spells."

"It's not just that, Protector. The wizard's spells are strong, but there's something stronger. I don't know what to call it, but it's calm and strong like a mighty mountain in the middle of a raging sea."

Mark frowned. He couldn't detect any spell other than Myrddin's. And he would have sensed it. "What are you talking about?"

"Like I said, I don't have the words to describe it. I didn't sense it before, maybe because I couldn't, or I didn't stay long enough, but I sense it now. It's—"

"Love. The word you're looking for is love," Myrddin said, coming out onto the porch to join them.

"What do you mean, Myrddin?" Mark asked.

"When I came to this land, I was running from them, the accursed. I suffered greatly at their hands, losing one nail bearer after another. This land gave me the opportunity to raise a family—a family that brought love to my heart and peace to my soul. It made my spiritual journey better. Our essence must have seeped into the atmosphere."

Lucilius nodded.

Mark frowned. How was Lucilius able to sense it? Did that mean he still had his powers or was this something else? He decided to shelve his questions until later; they had more pressing issues to handle.

"Can we harness it for the fight tonight?" Mark said.

"I don't know," Myrddin shrugged.

"And we know what to expect?" This time, Mark's question was directed at Lucilius.

"Asmodeus will come to annihilate everyone here. He will come with overwhelming force."

"So, in other words, more of those men in black suits," Mark concluded.

"We were able to handle it last time," Myrddin said.

"Because you caught him by surprise. Don't expect that edge this time around. He will come prepared," Lucilius cautioned.

Mark agreed. Their biggest drawback was numbers. Asmodeus had many more than they did, and if Lucilius was to be believed, the dude could make even more.

"We'll need more firepower," Mark noted.

Myrddin nodded.

"Can you...like banish the guy or something?" Mark wondered.

"Lesser demons, maybe. Asmodeus's hold on this plane will be too strong to cast him out," Myrddin said.

"Then we do what we do best...make it too costly for him to attack us anymore."

16

The plan was simple. Unlike last time, they wouldn't pull any punches; they would attack with as much combined power as they could muster.

Since they knew Asmodeus and his simulacra were susceptible to Gen's light, they planned on starting with that. She would be their secret weapon.

Their formation would be the same as the last time.

Gen, Mark, and Myrddin would face the onslaught while the rest of the group remained in the house.

Mark watched dusk arrive and waited with his sword over one shoulder and his MP7 strapped to the other.

They didn't have to wait long. It seemed that this time, Asmodeus didn't want any parley. Men in black suits swarmed the ranch and rushed at Mark, Gen, and Myrddin.

Mark looked at the simulacra in surprise. They were a lot more than last time. If each was just a fragment of Asmodeus's power, exactly how strong was the demon?

Myrddin clapped his hands together, and a containment field appeared around the ranch, cutting off the horde.

Gen released her powers, washing the ranch with blazing white light. None of the simulacra survived it washing over them. They screamed in agony and burst into specks of black particles. Mark's grin slipped when he saw hundreds more men in black suits slam into the containment field. With each pounding fist, a wavy shimmer of faint blue light illuminated the dome covering the ranch.

"Do we have enough juice to handle this many copies?" Mark asked Gen.

Gen looked at the mass of black suits surrounding the gate of the ranch, and she felt a thread of worry worm its way into her heart. She could burn every one of the demon's simulacra if given enough time to rest and recover her spiritual energy. "What do we do?" she asked her granddad.

"Myrddin, could we bottle them in?" Mark asked.

"What do you mean?"

"We could create a funnel with the containment shield. A gap we can control. That way, we can take turns at the clones. Reduce their numbers to a more manageable amount," he explained.

Gen wasn't sure she understood, but she noticed her granddad grinning.

"Gen can rest now. Create a gap, and I'll handle the suits that come through. The only way this will work is if we can control the containment shield. Create an opening and then lock the copies in," Mark said.

Mark removed the MP7 from his shoulder and stretched his neck. He walked a few feet ahead of Gen and Myrddin, grasping his sword in both hands.

"Now."

Myrddin chanted and rotated his hands. Gen watched as a section of the containment shield seemed to collapse, and the simulacra rushed in like a black cloud of insects.

Mark centred himself as the simulacra rushed at him. He could feel the sword humming, and he swung it in a wide arc, aiming for the middle of the simulacra. The metal blasted through the resistance of their bodies like a knife through butter. The simulacra screamed and exploded around Mark as he wove and danced through the mass.

He could feel the flow of the battle. He was an avenging angel wreaking havoc in the midst of the creatures. They died in droves. Many tried to run from his reach, but none made it out of the circle of death he created around himself.

Minutes later, he stood panting as the last simulacrum exploded into black dust.

He turned back and walked past Myrddin, nodding as their eyes met.

They could do this. No matter how many creatures Asmodeus threw at them, if they could continue to funnel the creatures into a narrow opening they could control and take turns fighting in, they could weather the storm and last the night.

Mark reached Gen's side and turned in time to see Myrddin create a firestorm that washed over the rampaging throng.

"This seems too easy," Gen said. Almost as though Asmodeus was testing their defences, she thought.

"It looks that way because we're coordinated, and they aren't."

"I still feel like something's wrong. Where is Asmodeus?"

"Hoping to wear us down?"

Gen didn't know why she felt uneasy. She scanned the sea of black suits, looking for their master.

He has to be nearby. Or can his clones function by themselves? Do they think? Gen wondered.

Mark frowned as he acknowledged Gen's point. Asmodeus had led the creatures during the last attack. Was he badly hurt from Gen's light, or was he waiting and biding his time?

If this was all that Asmodeus had to throw at them, they didn't even need to funnel the creatures. The containment shield seemed to hold them at bay.

Mark felt the attack coming before its negative energy slammed into the containment shield and shattered it into a million pieces.

The simulacra rushed into the ranch, and all hell broke loose.

Lucilius paced around the sitting room, angry that he was useless.

"I cannot sit idly by while there is a fight to be fought."

"Gen told us to stay indoors for our own safety," Isabella cautioned.

He grunted in reply and found himself walking toward the door. "You two really sit while the Nail Bearer fights for you?" he snarled at Josephine and O'Neal.

"What would you have us do? This is way above our heads," O'Neal retorted.

"You are God-touched. Use your powers and fight."

He reached the door and turned to face the people in the room again. "The enemy that seeks to devour us will not wait because you are hiding here. We need to take the fight to Asmodeus."

"It's safer in here. Gen's granddad said the shield will hold," Theo said. He also wanted to rush out and help Gen, but he remembered the last attack. Those things in human bodies looked evil, and he had felt helpless in the face of that.

The front door shuddered as a force slammed into it, and everybody in the room tensed. Silence filled the house as they waited to see whether the shield would hold.

241

"I told you the shield would ho—"

The front door shattered, and men in black suits flooded in.

Mark swung his arm and cut through a charging simulacrum, but another immediately took its place. They were yet to see Asmodeus, but the negative blast told them of his presence.

His arm felt heavy, and he knew his body was tiring.

They were superior to the creatures rushing at them, but their power seemed to be nothing against the mass.

Mark saw lightning burst out of Myrddin's fingers and obliterate simulacra, but still, an endless tide of creatures mobbed in. He ducked under a swinging claw that slashed and then attacked it. It fell and exploded, and Mark spun around and stabbed another that was trying to sneak behind him.

They had to keep fighting, or all would be lost.

Myrddin blasted creatures into nothing and pushed his spiritual senses as far as he could. Asmodeus was nearby, but his vision seemed clouded.

Could Asmodeus be blocking attempts at locating him?

Myrddin felt a sharp claw down his back and hit the protective shield he had around his body.

They were slowly but surely losing the fight.

The simulacra were simply too many.

Myrddin saw a group of over a dozen men in black suits rush at the front door of the house and slam into the protective barrier he had created.

At least the others are safe, Myrddin thought as he blasted another group away. He saw some trying to sneak up on Gen and dealt with them too. Gen nodded, grateful for the moment it gave her to recover.

Myrddin was surprised to hear the front door shatter as the simulacra burst through his barrier, rushing into the house.

The moment of distraction almost cost him as a creature grabbed onto his arm and tried to drag him down. He quickly created a spear of air with his free hand and stabbed the simulacrum in the head.

"They've gotten into the house," Myrddin shouted. He tried to move, but the men in black circled him like a swarm of angry wasps. He clapped his hands in fury, and a detonation threw them away from his body.

Myrddin prayed he would be able to get to the others in time.

Josephine screamed as the creatures in black suits rushed into the house. She didn't hesitate as she tried to recreate the feeling she had when she first used her ability. She remembered that she was scared, but more than that, she had wanted to stop the creatures from hurting her and the group.

She dug deep and pulled at her essence, and, as the creatures grinned in their eerie way and the nearest raised its claw to strike, the simulacra in the house froze.

Josephine heaved a sigh of relief and turned to the rest of the group, only to see that they, too, were frozen, looking like mannequins in a mall.

Theo had been reaching for his gun while stretching his other hand toward Isabella. Lucilius had a vicious sneer on his face, and he looked ready to take on all the black-clad creatures single-handedly.

Doctor O'Neal seemed to have a puzzled expression on his face and blinked at her.

Blinked at her!

Josephine stared in amazement as O'Neal turned in her direction and took a step.

How is he doing that?

Suddenly, he was moving at a normal pace, and Josephine thought her hold on time must have broken but saw all the simulacra still frozen in one place.

"How did you do that?"

"I...I'm not really sure, but suddenly, I could understand how you were freezing time...well, not exactly freezing it, more like slowing it down. Did you know that your time compression happens to be a bubble? The range isn't quite..."

"Not now, Doctor! How can you help?"

Josephine could feel the strain of holding all the simulacra in place. She wouldn't be able to hold them for long.

O'Neal was amazed. The air around Josephine bristled with vibrant colours that swirled and twirled. He didn't know how he knew, but it wasn't only that he could sense how Josephine's spell worked; he also just might be able to—

He stretched out his hand and placed it on Josephine's shoulder. He closed his eyes and concentrated.

There it is.

Josephine could twist a part of her reality and shift the area of compression. If she tugged really hard while bending that axis of time, there was the possibility that...

Ah, yes. That would do quite nicely.

O'Neal stretched out gently with his mind and touched the boundaries of the warp around Josephine. He nudged gently and spoke.

"You need to allow the flow of time to reverse in this direction."

"What are you saying?" Josephine strained to hold on. She could see the simulacra's faint movements—hardly noticeable but there all the same. She was losing control of her hold.

"Whatever you want to do, Doctor, better do it now."

245

"I can't do it. You'll have to trust me. Bend your will as I'll show you. Trust me."

O'Neal showed her, and she groaned with the strain of twisting time in a different direction. Reality resisted, the simulacra resisted, but her will was greater.

The simulacra began to reverse and herd backward. They moved out of the house, and the broken door corrected itself and became whole again. Josephine held on for as all as she could, and eventually, her hold snapped, and time flowed normally again.

She turned to see that the rest of the group were sitting down, except her and O'Neal.

Lucilius got to his feet and paced around the room.

"I cannot sit idly by while there is a fight to be fought," Lucilius said.

"Gen told us to stay indoors for our own safety," Isabella admonished.

Josephine stared at the people in the room and then at O'Neal.

"We went back in time?"

The doctor nodded.

"So that means...listen up, everyone. The creatures are going to break down the front door at any moment. We need to make a plan," Josephine said to the group.

The group stared at her in surprise.

"Gen's grandad said nothing would be able to enter in here, that we were safe here," Theo said.

"Well, that's not what happens. The door doesn't hold them. Whatever Gen's granddad did, it didn't work. We need to come up with a plan."

"Are you sure of this?" Lucilius asked.

Josephine thought of ignoring him but sighed. She didn't understand why Gen had welcomed Lucilius, and she wasn't sure she could get over her fear of him, but she would try to be civil—for Gen's sake. She looked at him and nodded, surprised to see he accepted her warning without any doubt.

"If the wizard's spell is insufficient, then we must prepare ourselves," Lucilius said.

"And how do we do that? The officer is the only one with a weapon. No offence, but we were put here because we're the weakest in the group. Our big guns are out there," Isabella said, pointing outside.

The door burst inward, and the simulacra rushed in again.

Myrddin blasted away the creatures as he struggled toward the house with fear gripping his heart. He knew he wouldn't be able to make it on time.

They had underestimated their adversary.

The simulacra were stronger than last time, and he hadn't compensated for that when he cast the runes on the door.

Light flooded the area around him, and every simulacrum near him burst into particles. He turned to Gen and nodded in thanks. He could see the strain on his granddaughter's face from expending too much spiritual essence.

Myrddin turned to the house when he saw the creatures reverse out. He sensed the displacement of power around the house.

Time reversal.

How was Josephine able to accomplish that in such a short time?

He could tinker with time, but he'd never been able to do that. It would have been a marvel if he could take time back, but the ability seemed beyond his grasp. And yet, here was a young girl reversing the flow of time.

Myrddin realized he had been distracted for too long when a claw slammed into his back. He grunted as he staggered. His shield was failing and, while the blow hadn't badly hurt him, he felt it like a little bruise.

He turned and slammed a gust of air into the creature snarling before him. The creature hit again, and they toppled together.

Myrddin quickly cast a spell, and a pillar of fire rained down on the simulacra struggling to get back up.

Where was Asmodeus in all this?

Mark panted as he kicked one simulacrum back and drove his sword into the chest of another.

The horde seemed endless. He had found his way to Gen's side, and they fought together as a team.

She had reduced the burst of her light to laser beams that shot out like high-projectile bullets and pierced the enemies' hearts and heads. Mark wondered if they even had hearts.

They were tiring. He could see it in the way Gen moved. Myrddin didn't react as swiftly to attacks—he could barely keep his hands up. And there seemed to be no end to the mass of black suits.

Mark ducked a lunge, reversed his sword, and pierced one of the creatures. His motions were instinctive now. His sword cut another simulacrum across the chest. Beams of light shot creatures away from him as Gen defended his back.

Where is Asmodeus?

Mark had a bad feeling about the attack. Though they were hard-pressed, Mark didn't think this was the demon's end game.

"We need to get to the house. We can defend ourselves better," Mark shouted above the snarling of the simulacra.

"The house isn't as protected as I thought. The creatures can get in," Myrddin yelled.

"What about the others? Won't they be in danger?" Gen asked and shot at a rushing creature.

Myrddin felt the energy displace again and looked to see another set of creatures reversing away from the house.

"Maybe the house will be a safer bet. Josephine's ability can help us greatly."

"Then let's retreat."

Gen flared brightly, and a radius of light slammed into the simulacra. The three ran to each other and formed a triangle with their backs touching.

Myrddin felt a portal opening at his right, and he slammed a torrent of fire into it. He felt his flame collide with a shield, and Asmodeus stepped through.

Gen blasted light at the demon, who stretched out his hand. A river of negative dark energy poured out and collided with Gen's light.

There was a detonation, and a backlash of energy slammed into everything around them. Mark staggered and fell to his knees. Myrddin stood rooted to the spot, but Mark could feel the burning of spiritual energy from Myrddin. Myrddin gripped Gen firmly to stop her from bowling over.

Asmodeus rushed at the three of them, and Mark quickly got to his feet, bracing himself. He caught Asmodeus's swing with his sword. There was a boom as both energies collided. Mark quickly shifted to a defensive stance as Asmodeus swung at him rapidly. Mark knew his sword could cut the demon but was also wary of Asmodeus's negative energy—one touch and things would be very bad for him.

Gen shot streams of laser light at Asmodeus. He deflected some with his sword, but others hit him. The demon didn't slow down, though. He deflected a blast of fire from Myrddin and kicked Mark in the knee.

Mark blocked the kick with the flat of his sword and saw smoke fizzle from Asmodeus's body at the point of contact.

Asmodeus shot out a wave of negative energy, and Gen met it with a shield of light.

"We need to do something," Gen shouted.

Asmodeus held his sword and smirked at them. "Not so mighty now."

"Glad you decided to show up. Didn't take you for a coward, hiding behind your clones," Mark taunted.

Asmodeus sneered and charged again.

Myrddin released another blast of fire at Asmodeus, but it slammed into the demon's shield. Shimmers of energy rolled off it.

Something seemed off, but Myrddin couldn't place it.

Asmodeus and Mark squared off and traded swift blows. Asmodeus was good, but Myrddin could see that Mark had the upper hand.

The fight would have been over if they weren't spent. They had expended a lot defeating the simulacra, and there were still so many of them.

Maybe, just maybe, they could still win the battle.

17

Josephine slumped as time flowed back to normal. She felt drained, as though she hadn't eaten for days. She had now reversed it three times, and the strain was telling. She didn't think she could do it again.

Which meant, if they didn't come up with a plan, things would go very badly for them.

Lucilius stood up and began to pace.

"Listen to me. We don't have much time before the creatures burst through that door. We need to come up with a plan." Josephine saw the group stare at her in surprise. She knew she wasn't one to give orders, but she had seen the next few minutes, and she was sure she didn't want to die.

Lucilius opened his mouth to speak, and Josephine interrupted.

"Yes, Lucilius, we agree with you. We can't sit idly by."

"We aren't…" Isabella started, but Josephine cut her off.

"We aren't safe here. The door isn't going to hold." Josephine turned to O'Neal. "Tell me you have something. I saw you staring into space throughout. What can we do?"

O'Neal looked at Josephine. "I can understand the truth of the sigils engrafted on the windows. I think I can adjust the lines to create a more potent rune."

"Good enough for me. We don't have much time."

Josephine and O'Neal hurried to the front door. The rest of the group followed and watched in surprise.

"What are you two doing? We shouldn't tamper with anything, guys. Remember what the old man said," Isabella cautioned.

"I agree with her. Gen's granddad knows what he's doing," Theo joined in.

"Look, I've seen it three times. This door fails, and the creatures get in. The last time, we were torn apart by their claws. I was barely able to reset the time. I don't think I have it in me right now to do it again."

"What are you talking about?" Isabella asked.

"She can reset time," O'Neal said as he studied the sigils crafted across the door.

It was a work of beauty and perfection, and O'Neal didn't think he needed to add anything; well, maybe just change this line to be more like this—O'Neal wove his hand and traced a new line over the existing marks. He concentrated and felt essence leaving his body.

He felt light-headed, but he didn't stop because their lives depended on it.

He didn't just want the door to be solid; he wanted it to be able to destroy anything that passed through.

Luckily, he didn't need to change the marks for the anchor. The sigil targeted undead and beings with negative energy. That was good. All he had to do was increase the power of the sigil.

O'Neal stepped back moments later and took a deep breath to steady his shaking hands. The change had taken more from him than he realized.

"Will it work?" Josephine asked. She didn't know what O'Neal had done, but she could sense a difference in the air around the doorpost.

O'Neal shrugged and said, "Only one way to find out." He opened the door as the simulacra rushed at it.

Josephine prepared herself to try and stop time, but she stumbled and leaned against the wall. Her eyes widened as she saw one of the men in black suits jump into the house.

There was a sizzling sound, and the creature exploded.

Josephine heard Isabella yelp in shock. More creatures rushed into the house and met with the same fate.

Josephine laughed.

They were safe.

They were winning the fight.

Asmodeus was strong, but he fought recklessly while Mark remained calm, the combat knowledge of the first protector giving him an added advantage. He moved with uncanny ease, dodging Asmodeus's swings at the last moment. The demon bled from numerous cuts, a dark brown stream oozing and smelling of sulphur.

Gen kept any stray simulacrum from attacking while Myrddin blasted away any group of creatures that planned to attack.

"Is this it, Mighty Prince?" Mark taunted. He wasn't sure if that was a smart move, but he was somewhat surprised. The last time he tangled with Asmodeus, he had felt the demon's strength. This time around, Asmodeus seemed uncontrolled, unco-ordinated, and unusually weak.

It must be due to the number of simulacra that he had created. Maybe the demon had spent more energy than it had initially planned?

Asmodeus swung, and Mark parried and rotated his sword, deflecting the blow. He moved quickly and stabbed, piercing the demon's thigh, and for the first time, Asmodeus screamed.

Mark raised his sword for another strike when Asmodeus wavered before him.

"Stop him from teleporting," Mark screamed at Myrddin.

The wizard chanted and slammed his hands together. A containment shield covered a small radius around them.

"It won't hold for long."

Asmodeus staggered away from them, and he wavered again.

Mark watched as Asmodeus's features underwent a drastic change. "No way."

His features rearranged, and Mark stared into the eyes of the shape-shifting Remus.

"What's going on?" Mark asked Myrddin.

Myrddin stared at Remus. "We've been played," he told Mark and Gen.

"Are you saying it's been Remus all along?" Gen asked.

"So it would seem."

"But how? The simulacra? The sword? The negative energy." Mark was confused. He watched Remus limp to one corner of the containment field. Simulacra slammed their claws on the shield, but it held, at least for now.

"I don't understand either," Myrddin admitted.

Gen took a step toward Remus and stopped. He held himself up with the aid of Asmodeus's energy sword.

"You don't have to serve him, Remus. You can be free."

"Free? I am free. I am greater than I ever was. I have eaten of his flesh and drank of his blood. My power is divine," Remus snarled.

"This isn't freedom, Remus. You can break free from their hold. Let me help you. Lucilius is free now."

"Lucilius is a traitor, and when we are done wiping you from the face of the earth, his punishment shall be a thing of legend."

"But you are here alone. Asmodeus left you here to die," Mark said.

Remus laughed at them. "Alone? I gladly offered to be here. You think this is the end?"

He continued to laugh, and Mark cast a worried glance at Myrddin and Gen.

Suddenly, a pillar of bright light struck the ground meters from Myrddin's shield and blasted every simulacrum around the pillar into particles of smoke.

The light faded, and a being walked toward the group. Every simulacrum around it exploded and died. The being walked through the containment shield, shattering it in the process, but no simulacrum attacked.

Mark felt the being's power wash over him, and the desire to quiver in awe overwhelmed him. His grip on the sword tightened, and he used it as an anchor to steady himself.

The being's light dimmed, and Baraqiel stood before them.

"We must make haste. Asmodeus seeks to devour your town."

"What?" Myrddin asked in surprise.

"This is but a ruse, a diversion. He has opened a portal to the underworld, and if he isn't stopped, this town will be no more."

Remus's laughter broke the silence that followed the angel's words. "He promised to destroy all you hold dear, Nail Bearer. Asmodeus keeps his promise."

"What do we do?" Gen asked.

"We need to separate. We can't allow Asmodeus to succeed," Mark stated.

Myrddin nodded. "I'll go with Baraqiel."

"I'll go too," Gen added.

"No, you and Mark remain here and look after the group. This is dark magic, and I think I'm the best suited for that."

Gen nodded reluctantly.

Baraqiel created a portal, and Myrddin turned to Gen and Mark. He nodded at them and walked through the portal.

Baraqiel glanced at Mark. "Feel the sword in your hands, Protector. It is a celestial weapon."

The angel stepped through the portal, and it snapped shut.

Mark looked at Remus and the swarm of simulacra creeping toward them.

Feel the sword.

He knew Baraqiel wouldn't leave them defenceless. That meant the angel believed the sword in his hands could change the tide of the battle.

Feel the sword.

Mark knew the sword was powerful, but it was a weapon to him—an enchanted weapon that could kill the forces of darkness.

Feel the sword.

"Buy me as much time as you can," Mark told Gen and shut his eyes. The simulacra snarled, and Mark heard Remus join them as they rushed.

Josephine leaned against the wall and tried not to doze off. The creatures had stopped attempting to enter the house, perceiving that the open door was a trap. O'Neal stood with a far-off look on his face, and Josephine wondered what was going on in his mind.

"I think we're safe now," Isabella said, and Josephine smiled. She had been helpful.

Lucilius still seemed ready to walk out of the house, but Theo was blocking the doorway.

"What do we do next?" Josephine asked.

"Next? We sit tight and wait for all this to be over. I'm not sure what I expected, but it definitely wasn't this. No one will believe me if I write any of this online," Isabella grumbled, and Josephine shook her head.

"I was talking to the good doctor."

Isabella glanced at O'Neal and turned to Josephine.

"I don't know what he saw when Gen touched him, but I think it messed with his mind. He's been not here *here*, if you know what I mean."

Josephine ignored Isabella's chatter. She was probably as nervous as every one of them, maybe except Lucilius, who was just upset that he had to sit this fight out.

O'Neal turned to Josephine after a moment and said, "There's a pillar of light on the ranch."

Everybody stretched to see if they could see through the doorway, but no one stepped outside.

Josephine didn't see anything, but she sensed a ripple in her spirit. The same feeling she had when Gen and Mark were in the barn with Lucilius.

O'Neal cocked his head to one side and listened.

"It seems this was just a distraction by the enemy. It looks like the town may be in danger."

Josephine groaned and struggled to stay standing.

They had to do something.

Mark felt Gen release her light and destroy the simulacra rushing at him. A grunt of pain from Remus told Mark he had just seconds to find out what Baraqiel meant.

Feel the sword.

He concentrated. He went into a meditative state and poured as much of his spirit as he could into the sword.

Feel the sword.

It was a flicker at first.

The sword seemed to throb to a specific beat. Then Mark realized it was his heartbeat.

A calmness came over him, and Mark saw the sword as it was.

He felt a soothing feeling wash over his soul.

Peace.

Kindness.

Joy.

Patience.

He felt refreshed. His spirit tingled with power, and he opened his eyes.

He saw the mass of darkness swarming toward him and Gen. He saw how low in essence Gen was. He saw Remus scream in rage as he pulled back his arm to strike.

Mark saw it all, and he wasn't bothered.

He was at peace, and he knew what to do.

The sword was more than a weapon. It was a conduit—a conduit to a greater and higher power. And Mark tapped into that power.

He stretched out and gripped Gen by the shoulder, transferring some of the power to her.

Gen snapped upright as energy surged through her. Her eyes blazed with light as it filled her spirit, and she released it out.

Mark felt more of the power surging from the sword, and he slammed the sword with the tip down into the earth.

Light blazed from Gen and the sword, and every darkness evaporated.

O'Neal felt the surge of power rushing toward the house. The simulacra that had waited for them to come out tried to run away, but they couldn't escape the tide of brilliant light that washed over them.

The creatures screamed in agony and blasted apart into dust.

Josephine felt the power wash over her, and she felt renewed with vitality. She stood straighter and looked around in amazement.

"What just happened?"

O'Neal smiled. "A divine intervention," he whispered.

Mark rose to his feet.

He felt great, better than he'd felt in a long time. He noticed Gen drawing back her power as wisps of black particles drifted away. No simulacra remained—every darkness had been banished.

Nothing remained...except Remus.

Remus whimpered on his knees in pain and anguish. His body shook in shock, and he had a dazed look in his eyes.

"What happened to him?" Gen asked.

"I can't tell, but it looks like signs of withdrawal. I've seen the same look from drug addicts and broken war veterans," Mark answered.

"What do we do with him?"

"Can you check to be sure there isn't any taint from Asmodeus or his former life?"

Gen nodded and bent down. She stretched out her hand and rested it on Remus's head.

A trickle of power left her, and she saw. She stood up and shook her head.

"He's normal. Broken, but normal."

"Can you...heal him?" Mark asked.

"I don't know, but now isn't the time. We need to get to town and help my granddad."

Mark nodded and turned in the direction of the house. He sensed the rest of the group coming toward them. He realized that his perception ability had grown. He could sense the spiritual energy of living animals meters away from him. There was a squirrel in its burrow outside the fence of the ranch. Further still, a fox? No, a dog roamed the streets ahead.

"Glad to see you're all okay. Even you, Lucilius," Gen said with a big smile when they reached the house.

Lucilius nodded and looked at Mark, then at the sword in Mark's hand. "You are different," he stated.

Mark realized that he was. He felt at peace—content with himself and his place in life. He also realized that he had been jealous of Lucilius. Jealous that he had been given a second chance after everything he had done. Mark was glad the feeling was gone from his soul. He nodded at Lucilius and turned to Josephine and O'Neal.

"Thanks for keeping everyone safe." He didn't know what had happened in the house, but he saw that Josephine stood with more confidence—the kind that could only come from experiencing a conflict and coming out victorious.

O'Neal stared at Mark and then the sword.

"This is truly a work of wonder." He stretched out and stopped a few inches from touching it. He couldn't see any runes or sigils, but the sword shone with brilliant light. He knew how it had been formed, but the sword seemed different. "It is perfect." O'Neal withdrew his hand.

"As much as we'd like to stay, we need to get to town immediately," Gen said.

"We heard. Asmodeus there, right?" Josephine said.

"How did...never mind." Gen shook her head and turned to Mark.

"Can your sword get us there?"

Mark looked at his sword. *What was Gen asking? Did she think the sword could teleport them to town? Could it do that?*

"I don't know, Gen."

Mark noticed O'Neal start to say something, but Gen interrupted him. "We need to get to town, Mark. My granddad's alone against Asmodeus."

"We're coming," Josephine said.

"Who?" Isabella asked.

"O'Neal and I are coming with you."

"I don't—" Isabella shook her head.

"Okay, but we need to leave now. The rest of you will remain inside till we get back."

Gen wondered why Mark wanted Josephine and O'Neal with them, but she shrugged off that line of thinking. More help would certainly be needed. She hurried to the van only hoping they would get to town in time.

18

Myrddin stepped out of the portal and into the town of Dundurn. He could already feel the wrongness in the air. They had arrived too late.

Buildings were shattered and destroyed. Bodies were scattered around.

He immediately began to weave spells in the air. He needed to prepare. If Asmodeus was here, he needed to be as ready as he could be.

He buffed up his shield and added another layer of protection, then weaved a sword of air and another of fire.

"Human blood has been shed. The portal is about to open. Prepare yourself, Guardian," Baraqiel said.

"Will you be by my side?"

"I will be where I'm needed, have no fear. Hold on as long as you can; help comes."

Myrddin nodded. He would do his best and stand as a bastion for humanity.

The night was silent. He walked to the centre of town, wondering if anyone had survived.

"I'm not sure I can create a containment spell so wide, Baraqiel."

The angel nodded, and, in an instant, Myrddin felt a containment shield go up.

"Can we block Asmodeus?"

"Not possible. He will only create another portal. We must face him here and now."

Asmodeus appeared as soon as the angel finished speaking. The demon stood behind a makeshift altar with blood spilled all over it.

"You are too late, mortal. The portal opens, and my brethren arrive." The portal behind Asmodeus shimmered with dark energy. A reptilian creature with bat-like wings flew out of it. "Your town shall reap the reward of your arrogance and pride," Asmodeus said. "This is merely the vanguard of a great and mighty army."

Myrddin ignored the bragging and aimed his sword of fire at the bat-like creature. It made contact, and the creature staggered back but remained unhurt.

Hmm, a creature of hell was most likely immune to mortal fire, Myrddin thought.

More of the bat-winged creatures poured from the portal. They assembled in front of Asmodeus, waiting for his command to attack.

"Do we have a host of your brethren waiting for our signal?" Myrddin asked Baraqiel.

"We will make do."

Myrddin sighed. He would have to hold the line for as long as he could till help arrived. He just hoped it would be soon.

At that moment, he heard the sound of an approaching van and smiled. It screeched to a halt beside him, and his family stepped out.

Gen rushed over and hugged him. Myrddin turned and saw Mark step out of the driver's seat. He looked different. *More mature?* He held his sword calmly and looked at the army of hell standing with Asmodeus.

"Mark, glad you could make it," Myrddin said with a smile.

Mark turned to him, and for a fraction of a second, Myrddin thought he saw particles of energy flicker in his eyes. Then Mark smiled, and the look was gone.

"Couldn't allow you have all the fun," he said. "What do we have here?"

"Asmodeus opened a portal to hell through human sacrifice. That's his army, and this is ours." Myrddin swept his arm to indicate everyone beside him.

Mark looked at the creatures lined up in front of Asmodeus. "Looks like uneven odds," he chuckled.

"We can only try our best," Myrddin tried to encourage Mark, whose grin widened.

"I meant for them."

Again, Myrddin saw the particles flash in Mark's eyes. *What happened at the ranch while I was gone?*

Josephine and O'Neal walked over. Josephine was shaking with terror, but she was also jacked up from the surge of power that entered her at the ranch. She felt like she could take on the world. "What's the plan?" she asked.

"Gen and I will take care of Asmodeus. You guys handle the rest."

"Well, not that I'm complaining, but isn't that a little presumptuous of you, Mark?" Myrddin asked.

"That is a brilliant plan," Baraqiel stated. "They can banish Asmodeus. Let us be quick before the other princes decide to take advantage of the portal," Baraqiel told the group.

"Ready for this?" Mark asked Gen, and she nodded. "Take us closer, Baraqiel," he told the angel and then centred himself. He felt the power of the sword answer his call, and he nodded.

A portal appeared, and Mark and Gen walked through.

Myrddin had to stop himself from rushing into the portal, too, to stand at Mark and Gen's side. He would stick to the plan and hope it wasn't a fool's gambit.

At Asmodeus's silent command, the creatures screeched and flew toward the group.

Myrddin felt Baraqiel move, and the first swarm ceased to exist. He didn't see the angel strike, only Baraqiel floating in the air in his majesty.

Power radiated from him in waves, destroying any creature foolish enough to fight him.

Maybe this will be easier than we thought.

Mark and Gen stepped out of the portal a few feet from Asmodeus.

"So, you stand as humanity's champion mortals?"

Mark nodded to Gen, and, without a word, he released all the power in his sword. Asmodeus created a shield around himself, but Mark wasn't targeting the demon. He knew he had to cut off any hope of reinforcements for Asmodeus. His power surged toward the portal and slammed into it. It shook and wavered in the air, and Mark poured out more power. He heard Asmodeus begin to shout, but it was drowned out as the portal exploded.

A backlash of incredible energy swelled out of the destroyed portal, and Mark slammed his sword into the earth. He created a counterpoint of energy, and the two slammed into each other, cancelling each other out.

Asmodeus moved with a speed that defied science, but Mark was ready. His sword clashed with Asmodeus's, and energy burst from the point of contact.

Gen used that moment to release light into Asmodeus's face.

His shield rose but shattered as Gen's energy hit it, and Asmodeus screamed as Gen's light washed over him.

Mark struck, slicing across the demon's chest, and light detonated in the cut. The force of the explosion flung him backward.

Mark spun his sword in the air and slammed it into the ground again. "Now!" he shouted.

He funnelled as much power as his body could hold and touched Gen's body. Gen opened herself to it, and it flowed into her. She blazed like the noonday sun, and the power lifted her off the ground.

"BEGONE!"

An explosion started from Gen and spread out.

Asmodeus's eyes widened in fear. He quickly opened a portal to escape, but Mark snapped his fingers, and the portal exploded.

The light and the power of Gen's word struck Asmodeus simultaneously, and neither his shield nor his body could withstand it; both were ripped apart.

The light and the word continued spreading through Dundurn, destroying every creature of darkness in its wake. The altar of human sacrifice evaporated into dust when the power struck it.

The night lay quiet, and Mark and Gen walked back to the group.

"That was...I have never..." Myrddin stammered. For the first time in millennia, he felt something in the centre of his soul. For the first time in a long while, the wizard realized hope welled up inside him.

"We didn't get to do anything," Josephine said, trying not to sound too disappointed. She couldn't help it; she thought they would need her, but they had taken care of Asmodeus by themselves.

"This is the part where only your ability can be of use, Josephine," Mark said.

She looked up.

"We can't allow the town and its people to die this way."

Josephine looked around. The scale of the destruction baffled her. "I don't think I can do it. And everybody here is already…"

"We'll help you out." Mark placed a hand on Josephine's shoulder to reassure her.

Baraqiel landed beside them and spoke. "The protector speaks well. I will lend my support, too."

When Mark saw the devastation Asmodeus caused, the first thing that came to his mind was Josephine's ability to reverse time. Maybe they could restore the town and save its residents.

The only challenge he saw was avoiding Asmodeus coming back to life as well.

"You know Asmodeus will also be revived," Myrddin voiced Mark's fear.

"That's a risk we'll have to take."

"I agree," Myrddin said.

"Remus will also be a problem for us," Gen noted.

Mark paused and looked to Baraqiel. "What do you suggest we do?"

"My counsel in this cannot be voiced," Baraqiel said.

Mark nodded. He wasn't surprised. They had to choose—their victory or the people's lives. Mark didn't think there was any debate.

"The townsfolk have to live. We will deal with Asmodeus and Remus again if we have to. At least we have the advantage of foresight. We know where they will strike and when they will strike."

Mark looked at everyone to see if there was any contrary opinion.

"There could be another way," O'Neal said. All eyes turned to the doctor, who continued to stare into the distance.

"What are you saying?" Gen asked.

"Josephine can create a point in reality where she focuses her timeline. But we will have to choose. If we save the people of this town, we cannot avoid bringing back Asmodeus, but we can avoid having Remus being as powerful as he was."

Mark considered the doctor's words. Having the people of Dundurn back was a sure deal. If they could avoid fighting Remus again, that would be a gain.

"Can you do what O'Neal said?" Mark asked Josephine.

"I don't understand a word of what O'Neal said, but if he knows what to do and when to do it, I'm good."

"Then, let's do this."

The group gathered together, and Mark clenched his sword in his hands. He felt inside himself and tapped into the ocean of spiritual energy the sword provided. He released the energy and held onto Josephine, who staggered as it flowed into her. She felt more alive than she had in her entire life. She concentrated and twisted time. A bubble formed around her and began to spread. Even with the power flowing into her, she felt the strain as it grew.

Josephine felt Baraqiel place his hand on her shoulder, and more power flowed into her. Gen and her granddad added their power, and Josephine felt like she could take hold of the sun and pluck it from the sky.

Her time bubble spread rapidly and covered the town. She turned to O'Neal. "Your turn, Doctor."

O'Neal continued to stare off into the distance, and Josephine opened her mouth to call out to him again when he turned to her. "I see it," he said. "The tangent point is here when a woman goes to feed her dog. We can make the dog come to the house a microsecond before she hears his bark from her kitchen. Do that, and we will have a new focus that we can build on."

Josephine released the power in her ability, and the damaged buildings began to jump back to their positions. Explosions reversed, and fires snuffed out. Asmodeus walked backward and entered a portal that was extinguished.

As Dundurn came back together, the burden on Josephine swelled, and she knew that without the others' support, there would have been no way for her to create a spell this powerful.

The moment came; a woman carrying a dog dish walked backward into her house wearing fluffy slippers and a shower cap over her head.

The dog trotted away from the woman's house, and Josephine allowed the time to flow back as normal. The dog walked toward the house, and Josephine jerked the flow.

The dog stuttered as it walked and, this time, arrived at the house a second later than it had originally.

"Done." Josephine felt drained as all the support from the others left her.

"How do we stop Asmodeus from destroying the town?" Gen asked.

"This is a different timeline. Asmodeus doesn't see the woman looking for her dog in the middle of the night, so he lacks a human sacrifice. He won't be able to channel his portal and will feel the loss of power when Remus is defeated. He will retreat to consolidate his power," O'Neal explained.

Gen smiled. "Then we have won."

Mark looked into the distance where he battled Asmodeus and clenched his sword tighter. There would be another day of reckoning for the prince of demons. He felt a soothing pressure as Baraqiel placed his hand on his shoulder.

"Be vigilant, Protector. You will battle the demon of fear again."

Baraqiel nodded, and a beam of intense light took him away.

"Couldn't he have taken us to the ranch before he left?" O'Neal asked, and Gen smiled.

"I'm sure he was called away for something very important," Myrddin said.

Mark continued to stare at the empty spot when Gen touched him on the arm. "We did good this time, Mark. We saved lives."

He turned to Gen and looked into her eyes. "We could have ended it here."

"It would have cost us too much. I know you know that. Let's go home."

She could see Mark had changed, but she was glad because it was for the better. He was still himself, but he felt more stable to her.

Gen held Mark's hand as they walked.

EPILOGUE

They took Remus to a psychiatric ward in Saskatoon the following day. Gen tried healing him, but anytime she reached out with her ability, she felt a resistance. No matter how much she tried, the feeling continued, and Gen concluded that maybe Remus wasn't meant to be healed. He was alive, but he couldn't speak, and there didn't seem to be anything behind his eyes.

When Gen and Mark came back to the ranch, they met the group in the sitting room.

"Some decisions have to be made, Nail Bearer," Lucilius said.

"You know my name is Gen, right? You don't have to keep calling me that."

"But that is who you are, Nail Bearer. What do you plan to do with all of us?"

Gen shrugged. She hadn't really thought about anything except surviving Asmodeus. Maybe they had a chance to live a normal life. "You can do anything you want, Lucilius. You are a free man."

"But they'll always be a place for you here should you wish it," Mark added.

Gen could see Mark's words meant a lot to Lucilius.

"You don't have to be in a hurry to make any decision, Lucilius," he added.

"Yeah, you can stay here with us," Isabella said.

Gen frowned. While she didn't mind having them around, she didn't think Isabella was in the position to offer anyone a place to stay. "For now, anyone who wants to stay is free to do so," she said. "But we will need to plan for the future. Do we all have to be in one place? Is that the best decision?" Gen said.

"I'm sure my aunt will be very worried. Maybe I'll stay with her for the time being," Josephine said.

Could she go back to teaching after all that she'd seen and done? Would she even want another life than the one she had now? She could reverse time, for goodness' sake. Was teaching really the best use of her ability?

"I'll stay here if that's all right with you," O'Neal said.

Gen nodded.

She hadn't known the doctor before, but whatever gift he now had, it seemed to have made him less sociable and eccentric.

For now, staying at the ranch seemed to be best for everyone.

Theo looked around the group. The past couple of days had made him realize that he didn't know what having a close-knit family felt like.

He loved his dad, and he was sure he loved him too, but it had always been just the two of them.

Staying at the ranch had made him feel as though he had siblings, something he was desperate for while growing up.

"I'll check on you guys once in a while," he said, leaving out his intention to keep an eye out for anything suspicious. With his police connections, he could keep the group up-to-date on anything happening and be a reservoir of information.

Gen smiled at Theo and turned to the group.

"I don't know what tomorrow has in store for us, but I've seen the power and strength in our unity. Regardless of where you are and what you do, remember that you have a home here."

"Have we had lunch yet?" O'Neal asked, and everyone laughed.

Gen was back in the field of wheat. She stood in the centre, surround by healthy, living wheat.

Further away from her, some crops were blighted and suffering from one disease or the other. Beyond the ring of diseased wheat, the field was scorched and blackened.

She saw a speck in the distance and shaded her eyes as she tried to make out what was approaching.

It grew larger, and Gen realized that it was a giant flying creature with fire spewing from its mouth, burning the field.

No.

Gen reached out with her power, and a shield surrounded the wheat closest to her. The creature flew closer, and she knew it would target the diseased wheat next. She tried to extend her shield to cover the diseased wheat, but it couldn't reach beyond the healthy crops. She cried out in frustration as the creature's fire consumed the diseased crops. Suddenly, her shield raced outward to the farthest end of the field, and the flames slammed harmlessly against it. The beast roared and flew away.

Sighing in relief, Gen turned to see that she wasn't alone. Hands rested on her shoulders and back.

A group of people surrounded her. She recognized the faces of almost everyone there: Mark and her granddad, Josephine and O'Neal. She started and realized she could see the faces of the remaining two people clearly.

Her team was complete.

Made in United States
Orlando, FL
16 April 2024

45874625R00157